TAK

D0872651

THE KINDLY LIGHT

Annie Darton's life was happiness itself, living with her father, the lighthouse keeper of Gannet Rock, until an accident changed their lives forever. Forced to move, Annie's path crosses with the attractive stranger, Zachariah Rudd. Shrouded in mystery, undoubtedly hiding something, he becomes steadily more involved in Annie's life, especially when the new lighthouse keeper is murdered. Annie finds herself drawn into the mysteries around her. Only by resolving the past can she look to the future, whatever the cost!

Books by Valerie Holmes
in the Linford Romance Library:

THE MASTER OF
MONKTON MANOR

VALERIE HOLMES

THE KINDLY LIGHT

Complete and Unabridged

LINFORD
Leicester

First published in Great Britain in 2004

First Linford Edition
published 2005

British Library CIP Data

Holmes, Valerie
    The kindly light.—Large print ed.—
    Linford romance library
    1. Lighthouses—Fiction
    2. Love stories
    3. Large type books
    I. Title
    823.9'2 [F]

    ISBN 1–84395–932–1

Published by
F. A. Thorpe (Publishing)
Anstey, Leicestershire

Set by Words & Graphics Ltd.
Anstey, Leicestershire
Printed and bound in Great Britain by
T. J. International Ltd., Padstow, Cornwall

This book is printed on acid-free paper

1

'Father, the light's fine, glasses done.' Annie walked carefully down the iron stairs to the room on the next level where they kept the charts, lamp parts and signals. She was surprised when he was not there, busy, readying the equipment for the stormy night again. One thing was sure, the forecast was bad and on this ragged, exposed north-east coast the new lighthouse had already saved nine men's lives and many boats from crashing on to the treacherous rocks.

'Father, have you ... ?' Annie thought she heard something or some-one fall heavily downstairs.

'Father! Are you all right?' Annie called out, but could only hear a faint murmur in reply. She carefully ran down the spiral staircase against the cold stone wall as it curved to the ground floor of the lighthouse.

'Father!' Annie cried out in shocked surprise as she saw his crumpled body lying still on the hard, flagstone floor.

As she reached the fifth step from the bottom, she nearly slipped herself as it was covered in oil or grease.

'What happened, Father?'

It didn't make sense. There was no oil lamp or can cast aside on the floor and both of them took pride in keeping a clean and safe light. The sturdy figure of her father lay spent and motionless on the floor in front of her.

She lifted his head in her hands.

'Father, what happened, can you talk?'

He seemed dazed. A feeling of panic rose up within her. She was used to saving lives and helping the injured but not her father. He was always there to tell her what to do and to use his strength. She propped him up on her knee, dabbing the small cut on his forehead with the fabric of her long skirts.

'Father.' Annie tried to keep her voice calm as she tried to sit him up. 'I need you to help me if you can.' She tried to prop him up against the wall and straighten out his legs. He did not flinch, but neither did he stir. Annie felt a fear like no other.

Annie ran to fetch two blankets and a flask of brandy. She wrapped them around him. Then she tried to get him to sip some brandy from a small flask. He didn't take it and for one horrendous moment Annie feared he had lost his wits in the fall. She had heard of a fisherman in town who took a heavy blow from a boom when out in a storm. He had not moved for over a year before he died.

'Father, listen to me!' Annie almost shouted at him in desperation. This couldn't be happening to him — to her. He must hear her and respond. 'We need help. I have to leave you. Pray to God, Father, and believe you will be all right. I shall return as soon as I can. Do you understand me, Father?'

His eyes were half shut. The line of his mouth, normally lifted in a smile or conversation was set in a crease. Annie felt her spirits sinking as she stared in the hope that he would suddenly smile and answer her, promising all would be well.

She waited for a moment for any sign of comprehension to what she had said, but there was nothing — until she lifted his hand to place it tenderly on his lap. Annie's resolve not to cry nearly dissolved as he squeezed her hand firmly. He was still there. She kissed his cheek.

'I'll be back as soon as I can, Father. You'll be fine — you're strong.'

He squeezed her hand once more. Annie forced herself to leave her strong, brave father alone, like a defenceless child.

She wrapped her long cloak around herself and stepped out into the strengthening wind. The sound of crashing waves breaking against the jagged rocks below the headland

4

echoed around her head. The icy, salty, sea air almost stung her face with its relentless force as it was carried on the wind. It took her twenty minutes walking hard into the storm to reach the first cottage at the edge of the small fishing village of Ebton. She hammered on the door and, as it slowly opened, was relieved to see old Maude's crumpled face.

'Father's had a bad fall. He needs help.' Annie was shivering. She did not know many people in Ebton but Maude and her sister, Nellie, knew everyone and everything that happened thereabout.

'Nellie! Nellie!' Maude shouted to her sister.

The two old women soon had Annie reluctantly inside their cottage. Maude rang a bell and two men appeared within minutes from the inn.

Annie refused to stay with the elderly sisters.

'Leave it to the men folk, lass,' Nellie shouted, but Annie ran after Seth and

Amos Barton as they headed for the lighthouse.

'Send Culby with the cart,' Seth shouted back to Nellie, his voice carrying on the wind.

Annie and her father had always been outsiders to this small, tight-knit community but she was always touched by the way that they all pulled together in a crisis. This time, though, the crisis was her father.

⋆　⋆　⋆

'Annie.' The voice of Maude carried to her ears as the old spinster shuffled along the fine sand beside her. 'Do you think Ned King will dare show his face here, eh?'

'Why ever not?' Annie whispered back, wondering why the new keeper of the lighthouse should stay away.

Despite the personal contempt she herself felt for the man, Annie did not know of any reason why he should not attend Seth Walsh's funeral.

Two years had passed since her father had lost his job and nearly his life on the dreadful night of his fall. Without hesitation, the governing body had pronounced him unfit to keep his job.

Ned King was the third replacement the lighthouse had had since then. No explanation had ever been found for the spillage on the step. His accident had been put down to his failing health. That infuriated Annie because her father had always been fit, strong and reliable. Someone had done it, but who?

Annie Darton followed the cortege as it slowly made its way across the flat, sandy bay between the two fishing villages of Ebton and Scarbeck. She looked ahead of her and saw the coffin bearers sway right and left as they trudged across the beach.

Maude's eyes lit up as her chance to spread the latest town gossip further presented itself. Annie and her father were respected in Ebton. The old lighthouse keeper and his daughter had only recently rented Maude's sister, Nellie's, cottage so they were, in many ways, still as outsiders to the centuries-old fishing community.

'Word has it, that he let the light go out in the storm.' Maude gave Annie her most disapproving look as she wrinkled up her already-lined face.

Annie pulled her cloak around her tightly, and tilted her bonnet forward to try to shelter more of her raven-coloured hair from the icy dampness of the sea fret. It was nothing to the chill that ran down Annie's spine as she heard Maude's words.

In all the years that her father had managed the light, neither he nor Annie would ever have been so negligent as to let it fail in a storm. A keeper was paid to light the lamps a half hour before sunset and to keep them burning till near sunrise, checking on them every few hours throughout the night. On a stormy night they were expected to stay in the light-room all night long.

'Hush your mouth, you old gossip.

Have you no respect for the dead?'

Nellie's sharp reproof to her sister caused Maude to look humbly, yet defiantly back at Seth's widow and coffin as they continued the slow walk towards Scarbeck.

'I'm only a year older than yourself, Nellie,' Maude replied.

The two shared one fisherman's cottage by the inn and rented out the adjoining one. Nellie had lost her husband some fifty years since. The two fought and gossiped continuously, each loving every minute of it and, Annie suspected, had a hand in more things than it was provident to know about.

It was a three-mile walk from their home at Ebton to the church of St Cuthbert's at Scarbeck. Like the new lifeboat that could have saved Seth Walsh's life, Ebton also waited for the day it would have its own parish church. In the meantime, men like Seth Walsh died needlessly.

Although Annie could hear the waves lap upon the shore, the sea was lost in the now dense fog. She looked to the sandy, grass-covered dunes to see if her father was waiting to join the small group of mourners as they made their way up through the snicket between the dunes and the start of the cliff path.

Widow's Walk was what the locals called the pathway up to the church because it had seen many a widow mourn the loss of her husband whose life had been taken by a cruel sea. North-easterly gales, jutting headlands and ragged cliffs made this a treacherous coast.

One more danger hung around the shoreline like a silent storm that no-one mentioned or witnessed openly — smuggling. Most of the people had a part to play in it until last year when Jebidiah Vickers became involved. Now they were scared and careful as to what they said.

Annie thought she saw someone approaching through the mist, but wasn't sure who it was because the figure was standing tall and straight, unlike her father.

'Halt!' Archibald Grimethorpe, a dour figure, commanded from in front of the coffin. Her eldest son, Amos, supported Betty, Seth's widow, as the bearers were told to turn for the ascent up Widow's Walk.

Annie felt they were now in a race in time against the heavy mist. Moist, grey gusts already blew across their way ahead. They added to the gloom-laden atmosphere that surrounded the mourners.

Where was her father? She wondered why he wasn't waiting for them at the snicket, like he said he would be. If he had made his way up to the cliff path to stare at his beloved lighthouse, she knew he could be in danger. Since his fall, which had resulted in the lighthouse authority taking away his job as the keeper of the Gannet Rock Light, he had frequently returned to the cliff path to watch it, despite his injured leg and the presence of the latest keeper, Ned King.

Annie remembered the pain of those two first months as he gradually recovered from the fall. She had taken him to his sister's country house. He had been allowed to stay in a back room whilst he recovered from the fall, unseen and unobserved. He was below the company that she kept in her society since marrying above her station to a prosperous mine owner.

The drone of mourners could be heard now above the high-pitched calls of the scavenging seagulls that nested amongst the many clefts, ledges and caves. Annie wondered if she should leave the procession and seek out her father. The thickening grey cloud cover ensured no sun penetrated the dark and sombre day.

Annie stepped out of line to climb the cliff path, when she saw Reverend Josiah Armitage Marchbank waiting to lead the cortege as it joined the coast road.

The cold air, coupled with the haunting sounds of a psalm, added to

Annie's general sense of unease and foreboding. Hesitating, she looked from the figure of the demure priest, to the path, wondering what she should do, when she saw, slowly forming out of the mist and appearing like dark haunting spirits, the shapes of her father followed by Ned King. Annie was so relieved to see him safe and well as they carefully descended the cliff path.

The cortege continued at a steady pace, swaying gently, but never faltering on the soft sand as it gave way to the firmer, well-worn ground of the snicket, pausing only momentarily to join the reverend, who would lead them to the old church of St Cuthbert's.

Those who had the money had already prepaid for their one-way ticket in the Ebton hearse for their final journey. Poor fishermen's families, even if they'd lost their life trying to save others, still had to suffer the pain and exhaustion of this age-old tradition of trudging along the beach.

'Father,' Annie said quietly, as he joined them.

He patted her arm gently and fell into step next to her. Ned King hung back and rightly so in Annie's estimation. Maude's accusations echoed in her head, if he had neglected the light and subsequently caused The Merry Mermaid to run on to the rocks, then Seth had died unnecessarily in the subsequent rescue. Annie saw Amos Walsh spin round. His face, already reddened with grief, now positively glowered with anger and hatred as his emotions visibly rose to the surface, unabated.

'The nerve of the man! I'll send him to hell and back!' Amos started shouting, pushing through the procession to confront King.

Annie's father immediately blocked his path.

'No, lad. You're grievin', boy. Take your breath slow and easy and continue in the manner of the day.'

'Aye! I'm grievin' and he knows why!'

Amos pushed forwards towards the calm King.

'Not here! Not now!' her father said quietly and raised a firm but friendly hand to halt Amos and gestured for him to return peaceably to his mother.

Amos looked down at her father.

'His time's coming, Samuel — and soon!' He snapped out the words and then returned reluctantly to his mother.

On the night of the violent storm, the tide had whipped the waves so high that they had even breached some of the old fishermen's stone cottages in the bay. Before all its menace was complete, three families had lost their homes. Many people had cause to grieve for the resulting destruction of that night. Perhaps, Annie thought, her father was also unaware of the rumours about Ned King and presumed he was unjustly being made into a scapegoat for the resulting wreck and disaster. She decided to speak to him later and put him right.

Annie stood silently next to her

father as Amos rejoined his sobbing mother. Whenever the sea took a man's life, it was a terrible loss for his family. Fortunately, Betty Walsh was well provided for as she had three strong sons, all fishermen who would keep her out of the dreaded poorhouse — that is if they did not suffer the same fate as their father.

Annie glanced back and noticed a figure walking through the heavy mist. He was tall, and carried a bag slung over his shoulder. She knew she had to move forward yet couldn't help peering back at this stranger. Annie presumed he was one of Seth's distant relatives. She had no idea if he had any, as not many people in the village mixed beyond the towns around the bay. She was going to tap her father's arm but could see the pain in his face as he stared fixedly on the coffin ahead.

For a fleeting moment she felt a stab of pain in her own heart. Annie remembered when, as a young girl, she followed such a procession. Numb with grief, she hadn't spoken for nearly three months after it, until she came to terms with the loss of her beautiful and loving mother.

Annie tried to see if the stranger had caught up any distance. Perhaps he was just lost, or connected with The Merry Mermaid in some way. Something about his stature made him look like a man of the sea, not a fisherman, but a sailor.

She watched the procession move on, but could not resist one more glance back to study him again.

When she looked, he was nowhere to be seen. He'd disappeared. Annie stopped and stared hard into the mist, but there was no sign of him. Then she realised as the sound of the psalm was fading that she would have to run to catch up with the funeral. Fortunately, when she tripped on her long skirt as she ran, it was her father she stumbled into.

Unnoticed by the tiring procession, her father straightened her up and grunted quietly, 'Annie! Take care!' Only Ned King had seen and heard him, and his smile, or grimace, was of no comfort or consideration to Annie. She loathed the man. He had taken her father's job, but if that were not reason enough to dislike him there was more. She felt ill-at-ease whenever he was around. He leered at her, as if trying to see through her clothes to her skin. The thought made her flesh creep. Tall and handsome he may be, but his eyes had the depth of the darkest silent pool. Dangerously enticing — but deathly cold.

Annie walked on, head bowed. She glanced around to the cliff path one last time as they passed by, and there, sitting halfway up surrounded by marram grass, shrouded in the mist, was the mysterious figure of the stranger.

2

Once seated in the old Norman church of St Cuthbert's, Reverend Marchbank gave a good and lengthy sermon in honour of Seth. His widow sat proudly listening to his virtues — brave, generous, hardworking and proud — being extolled. Amos stared ahead of him at the coffin.

Nothing was said of the man's wild drinking, his temper, or of the many nights his sons had carried Seth, drunk, back to his long-suffering wife. Annie watched the grief on the faces of his three sons; no matter what his virtues or his vices were, he was, or had been, their father.

When, outside, the coffin was finally lowered into the ground, its final resting place, Amos's gaze fixed firmly on Ned King. The man seemed unaffected by the hatred in his eyes, whilst everyone else shuffled uneasily at the thought of a fight ensuing the funeral. It was Samuel, Annie's father, who broke the deadlock by walking Ned to the cemetery gate. Meanwhile, Annie paid her respects to Amos and his family before following on behind her father.

It was the stranger who distracted her attention again, as she followed the path around the corner of a large tombstone. She almost tripped over him as she cut across the grass in order to catch Samuel up more quickly. He was kneeling on the damp grass, head bowed in his hands.

Annie gasped, embarrassed and surprised, feeling awful as she had clearly interrupted a very personal moment. She realised she was standing on the grave he was paying his respects to and quickly stepped off it.

'I beg your pardon. I didn't see you . . . I mean . . . '

Annie straightened her bonnet and shawl nervously.

'That's all right, miss. No harm

done.' His deep voice surprised her.

When he stood to his full height he was quite tall, with a tanned skin, which seemed to tell her she was correct about him being a man of the sea. He looked strong and worldly. His eyes, although dark, were gentler than Ned King's. Annie was surprised by her reaction to this stranger.

Annie neither knew what to say or do, so she smiled politely, nodded and walked on. This time she fought desperately against the temptation within her to look back.

Her attention was quickly diverted as the figure of Amos ran past her at such speed he caused her to side-step to keep from being knocked down. Following closely behind him were his two brothers. The reverend ran next with his damp skirts flying wildly about his ankles. When the women appeared walking briskly along the pathway, Annie decided, forget decorum, and ran after the men.

Amos approached Ned swinging

wildly at him. King ducked calmly. Not much was known about him other than he had a London accent. But here, by the church gate, he was displaying an aptitude and knowledge of street fighting, although Annie had to admit he was avoiding Amos's angry blows rather than striking out at the distressed young man.

'Gentlemen! Gentlemen! This is neither the time, nor the place.' The reverend's voice pleaded with both men to calm down. It was only when Amos's two brothers pulled him back to his mother that peace ensued once more.

'Whatever your differences — in the name of God and in respect to your dearly departed father — cease this action, this minute!'

Amos was standing defiantly, glowering at King, but listened respectfully to the reverend's plea.

Ned doffed his hat and walked away calmly.

'You swine! Your time's coming, you murderer!'

His family drowned out Amos's threats as they tried to still his temper.

Meanwhile, to Annie's despair, it was her father who again followed Ned, leaving her with no alternative but to do likewise. Behind all the mayhem, the stranger leaned against the corner of the church looking on, impassively.

No-one seemed to notice his presence, except her. Their attention was fully focussed on Amos and his latest outburst.

'Don't take the lad's threat to heart, Ned. He's full of grief and you're a stranger to these parts.' Her father leaned on his walking stick and smiled genially at the younger man, King.

Ned's eyes were fixed pointedly on Annie as she approached. He didn't even look at her father as he replied, but eyed her up and down in a sickeningly intrusive and personal way.

'Not to worry, Samuel. Once he's wet his throat at the inn, he'll get over it. He's just flexin' his muscles and

showin' who's head of the household.'
Ned stared Annie straight in the eye,
almost trying to challenge her to stare
him out. 'We haven't had the chance to
become better acquainted, Miss Darton
— Annie,' he said.

'No. We haven't!' Annie snapped
back. She could not help herself from
answering in an unaffected, impolite
voice.

'Well, we'll have to put that right
then, won't we, Annie?'

Samuel's reply almost shocked
Annie. The sooner she told him about
the light going out, the better. His
normally shrewd character had obviously been affected by his fall, Annie
thought to herself.

'We shall call on you soon. It would
do us both good to see inside the old
lighthouse again. Eh, Ned?'

Ned nodded, giving no indication of
whether he thought it was a good idea
or not. Without volunteering a time or
another word he left them to return to
the lighthouse.

Annie walked over to the cliff edge and looked out across the now calm sea as it gently withdrew from the shore. The mist had lifted whilst they were in the church. She loved watching the sea's changing moods. It could be unpredictably violent in a storm or gentle, hardly giving the impression of moving at all, like today.

Yet, underneath the apparently calm blue-grey surface, strong dark currents moved like demons, waiting to pull any unsuspecting victim down into its murky depths. Standing off the cliff path, wrapped in her shawl against the chill of the breeze, Annie's heart felt heavy as she thought of the victims of the latest wreck to hit the rocks.

It was true that more would have been lost in the storm, had it not been for the fishermen's rescues and the light, but any life lost because of negligence, to Annie, was a great sin — a life that should have been saved.

'Home, lass.' Her father greeted her with his usual smile and warmth.

'They'll be waitin' on us returnin' at the cottage.'

Annie stepped back on to the safety of the coastal path where her father was standing, shaking his head in dismay at his headstrong daughter.

'You know better than to go off the pathway. This ground could crumble beneath yer feet, or one good gust of wind would blow you away to sing with the mermaids. Have you no sense or fear, Annie?'

He scowled at her, but as usual she just beamed at him and kissed his forehead just below his non-existent hairline.

Samuel Darton had a weather-worn face from years of being exposed to the salty sea air. Only a few wispy grey hairs escaped atop a shiny, sun-kissed head. Annie, with her mass of long dark hair stood a head taller than her father's strong but stocky figure. She loved him dearly but felt annoyed with him for seemingly encouraging Ned King's advances to her.

'I'll not have you matching me, Father. Certainly not to the likes of Ned King!' Annie put a defiant hand firmly on her hip.

'You, milady, should have stayed in York with your aunt. If only you'd let her guide you, you could've been married to a fine . . . '

Annie started walking along the pathway as it descended back down and round to the sandy beach, trying to ignore the familiar lecture he had spouted at her frequently in the last year. She had no wish to marry some spoiled city male, whose moods and manners were as unpredictable and unyielding as her precious sea. Annie loved her father dearly, but whilst they were on the path and away from the people of the town who would be approaching towards the beach below, she turned around defiantly.

'Father, I will not be matched to a total stranger. On that I am determined. If you weren't welcome there then I do not wish to stay under her roof.' Annie stifled a grin. 'Besides, as Aunt Amelia has pointed out, at twenty-four I am now past my preferred age. I am too practical and not good enough for the genteel folk she mixes with. I do not want to get saddled with an old soldier and spend endless hours trying to do embroidery whilst listening to his renditions of the day he came face to face with Napoleon!'

'Aye, tryin' would be right!'

Her father was chuckling to himself, as he was only too aware of Annie's domestic shortcomings. She could mend a shirt and darn a sleeve, but the finer aspects of needlepoint were beyond her patience, if not her ability.

'Perhaps you should listen, for a change. Many of our fine men have fought long and hard against Napoleon. They should be able to come home and relax with their wives, who should listen to their exploits with pride. Another thing, Amelia gave me good care after my accident, so I'll thank you not to be disrespectful to her.'

'Oh, Father, I know Aunt Amelia thought Colonel Sanderson was my last and best chance at marriage, but I ask you!'

Annie threw up her hands in outrage. When her father laughed at her she folded her arms and stared at his face. She was farther down the path than he, so for once she had to look up at him.

'And,' Annie raised her voice to stress her point, 'shouldn't the government ensure all of our soldiers return to jobs and a home? Aunt Amelia couldn't wait to have you out of there in case anyone found out you were her brother, a common lighthouse keeper, and not her act of charity.'

'Colonel Sanderson was well connected, Annie — a man of means. You could've had anything you wanted, if only you'd . . . ' Her father looked around him as if searching for the correct words to say. ' . . . tried a little, and please leave politics to the men folk, lass.'

Annie was quick witted and was

never at a loss for words. She knew it was the thing that had scared off most of her would-be suitors. Her aunt had been driven to the end of her patience by Annie's ploys to turn every single one of them away. It seemed that a pretty young niece was acceptable to flaunt, but not her weather-worn, semi-invalid father. She felt as though she were being used to attract rich old men into her aunt's house. Social connections meant nothing to Annie.

'If only I'd tried to pander to the whim of an older man,' Annie retorted.

'Isn't that what you came back here to do?'

For once Samuel Darton's reply was swift and startled Annie. She never thought of her father as being old.

'No!' Annie stared straight into his pale grey eyes. They looked tired, yet, until now she had never really noticed; with the exception of his fall, he had always had excellent health.

'At least with the colonel you would've lived in comfort,' he continued.

'I do,' Annie replied defensively. 'Why should I leave politics to men when they make such a mess of it?'

'Annie Darton, the mouth on you would scare off a saint!' Her father shook his head in a despairing gesture. 'In a life of luxury I mean, and then you could've had babies of your own.' Her father flushed as he blurted out the last comment in a rush as if they were words that should not have been spoken between a father and daughter.

'Oh, Father, I don't want his sort of luxury. I'd be no more than a dressed-up trinket for him to show off to all his younger army friends. I'd hate it.' Annie wrinkled up her nose at the thought. It was a childish habit, but one which her father always grinned at.

'You'd be a beautiful one at that, lass,' Samuel said proudly.

She put her hand gently in his.

'Perhaps, but I couldn't abide the thought of him pawing at me. He was far too old and, anyway, he may not be able to still make children.'

Annie had spoken sincerely, voicing the real reason why she could not bear to be alone with the colonel. In truth, his advances had scared as much as repulsed her.

Her father gasped. 'Annie Darton — you are beyond hope!'

He pulled his hand away from hers.

'You brought the subject up.' Annie did not see why he should think she could have children by such a man and yet not be allowed to express her disgust at the thought of a match between them. Surely, she thought, attraction should be equally important to both husband and wife.

'I did no such thing, Annie Darton.' He pushed past her and started descending the steepest part of the path, as if to escape quickly.

'You mentioned having children,' Annie continued unabashed. 'When I marry it will be for love, or I won't marry at all!'

'Well, my girl, you'll most likely be an old maid then, and a sad waste of humanity at that.' He did not stop, but continued down until the path met the flat sand by Widow's Walk. Annie watched the back of his bald head as he neared the beach below.

'So be it then. Aren't you fortunate?' she asked.

'How is that?' he shouted back to her.

'Because until I meet the man of my desires, I can look after you.'

Annie laughed because now his duty as a concerned father had been expressed; she knew that deep down he loved having her with him.

3

As they walked back to Ebton before the tide came in, she told her father again about Ned and what Maude had said regarding the light going out.

'Gossip is dangerous, lass. You should know better than that.'

'Why are you so keen to defend him? Why encourage his attentions? I'm sure I don't want them. I tell you, he's no good, and that's not gossip. That's my instinct.' Annie was surprised that her father merely shrugged his shoulders dismissively at her comments.

'That may be, but it doesn't do to make enemies, now, does it? Besides he is manning it on his own. I had you covering as my assistant. Until the Stockyards find him someone, he will be having his work well and truly cut out for him. There will not be many volunteers at the moment, I tell you.'

He did not look at her. Annie started to get the strongest feeling that her father was up to something — but what? He wasn't going to tell her what it was, that was for sure. If he was not blinded to Ned King's failings, then why did he go to such lengths to befriend him?

'Why, Father?' Annie persisted.

'Because, Annie, you know that Selwyn Fletcher's gang has been increasingly active along these shores. They've joined Jebidiah's men. Neither wants a light shining on their illicit activities. I have heard they've been linking up with another gang to the south, even harder men. Ones that would delight in a wreck or two.'

Annie was silent as her father's words penetrated her consciousness.

'Wreckers, here? The villagers aren't like that. They're honest fisher folk. They wouldn't stand for it!'

'Hush your mouth, girl. I shouldn't have told you. Wouldn't they? You're so naïve. Anyhow, the long and short of it is that any man who stands for the light now may have little choice as to who their master truly is. These are not happy times, lass.'

He shook his head and placed a comforting arm around Annie's waist as they approached the old cottage that was now their home.

She stopped as a horrid thought crossed her mind.

'Father, your accident — the fall. It wasn't an accident, was it? They did it, didn't they?'

He laughed — a loud, artificial laugh.

'No, lass. Aye, it was no more than an accident — just an old fool who tripped over his own feet. You have too good an imagination for your own sanity. Now stop this tittle-tattle. We appear to have a visitor.'

Annie looked up to the cottage; a fire was burning within it as smoke filtered out of the chimney atop its pantile roof. Maude appeared at the doorway.

'You made good time, Maude,' Samuel said lightly.

'Oh, we got a lift back on the blacksmith's cart. He was passing and took pity on two old women.' Maude walked off towards town laughing.

'Speak for yourself, Maude.' Nellie laughed a high raucous laugh. 'You're to have a visitor for a day or so. I've rented the loft room. He'll be no bother, and he'll help you pay your rent for a few days, perhaps longer.'

'But who is he? Why can't he stay in your loft room?'

Annie spoke out and then wished she hadn't as her father glowered at her and Nellie spun around. Annie knew it didn't do to cross her, but she was used to privacy and having their own space. It was a luxury, she knew, yet one she fought for stoically.

'You are not the owner of the cottage. I am! I do not have to rent out my space. You do!' Nellie poked a scrawny finger into Annie's shoulder.

Annie knew she had a valid point, but she found it hard to bite her lip and not respond once more.

Nellie sniffed the air defiantly, then turned her sweetest smile to Samuel.

'You have no objections, Samuel, do you?'

'No, Nellie. I'm grateful to you for the hospitality you have already shown us. The poorhouse would be a far less commodious place.'

Annie knew there was a very strong and poignant message in his words.

'Ladies.' The deep voice made Annie spin around as the stranger appeared behind her from the beach. 'Sir,' he continued as he saw her father, 'I hope I will not inconvenience you too much, or indeed for very long.'

'No bother, I am quite sure, Mr . . . ?' Samuel asked.

'Zachariah Rudd, sir.' He shook her father's hand firmly. He then removed his hat and addressed Annie. 'Miss.'

Annie had been drawn to this stranger since his first almost mystical appearance. She wondered how to respond now that he was to sleep under the same roof as her.

'Nellie! Nellie! Come quickly.'

Maude returned running as quick as her legs would carry her.

'What is it, Maude?' Nellie asked.

'Ned King . . . he's dead!'

'How, Maude?' Nellie asked.

'Well, Biddy Wilkinson heard from old Harold Blenkinsop that he was seen swinging off the light when the lassies were gathering flithers by the lower rocks.'

Nellie and Maude crossed themselves.

''ave they cut him down, Maude?'

'Ay, Nellie. The yeomanry was sent for. He's been placed in the chapel. No-one will go in the light now, for sure his soul will never rest. Will it, Nell?'

Nellie glanced down then looked at the stranger.

'You must forgive our manners. Annie, take yer lodger in and make him at home, lass.'

Annie wanted to listen to the gossip as much as everyone else did and hated being dismissed, but her father nodded to her and she obeyed. No doubt he would tell her later if more was said. Annie decided it was the stranger that they didn't want listening, and not her. Reluctantly, she opened the door to the simple cottage and entered.

She stoked up the fire in the hearth, placed the kettle over its grate, then turned to look at the stranger as he shut the door behind him and dropped his bag to the floor. For a moment she stared, confused. Here she was in the presence of a handsome stranger, alone, save for the door that separated her from her father and propriety. His dark hair and sun-kissed skin gave him almost a foreign appearance.

In the centre of the open cottage was an old oak table with a rough assortment of four wooden chairs around it. At one end was her father's bed and his table on which he kept his pipe and Bible. An open ladder led up to the loft room, normally a place where children would sleep if this had been a family cottage. It was where

Annie slept; it was her own cosy space, not up for rent, or so she had thought.

'Miss Darton, I apologise for burdening you and your father, but I assure you that I shall only be here one night, two at the very most.'

He smiled broadly at her, and stepped forward towards the fire.

His presence unnerved her. They both glanced at the small window and saw the two old women and her father in a huddle outside. The conversation was quite animated and Nellie, in particular, looked very concerned.

'I appear to have arrived at Ebton at a sensitive time.' Zachariah Rudd looked down at Annie, his smile had gone but his face showed concern.

'What brings you to our small hamlet, Mr Rudd?' Annie asked as she poured him a warm drink.

'Thank you,' he said gratefully. As their hands touched fleetingly when she gave him the tea, she felt how cold his were.

'You have been out a long time in the

cold. Why did you not go to the inn?' Annie asked, looking straight into his eyes, dark as Whitby jet. Annie could never look at Ned's eyes, on the few occasions she had been close to him, feeling repulsed. Rudd was different, but something about him made Annie feel he was not as straightforward as he would appear to be.

'Yes, I have.' He glanced at the flames of the fire. 'In more ways than one.' He almost muttered the words to himself. Then, as if he had forgotten himself, 'I wanted somewhere quiet, out of town, to stay for a night, until I can go to the hall.'

'Sunnington Hall?' Annie asked.

'Yes.' He looked back into the fire. 'I understand Benedict will return tomorrow or the day after.'

'You know Squire Benedict Stockyard?'

Annie did not mean to sound nosy, but the familiarity of the way in which he had called Mr Stockyard, Benedict, surprised her.

'Oh, it's a long story, but it will soon be sorted out — tomorrow hopefully. This Ned King, did he have a number of enemies here?'

'Does he!' Annie responded sharply. She disliked King intensely and felt a little stab of guilt that the man had met such a sudden and horrific end.

'Well, he seemed to be at the centre of a rumpus at the church and then, to be found in such a manner, it does hint at the very least that someone didn't like him.' He raised a quizzical eyebrow at her.

Annie bent over the unmade palette.

'Obviously so. I wouldn't know.' She did not look at him. One thing she had learned from Maude and Nellie was that it paid not to see and say, about some things at least. Sometimes in the night, she could hear movement outside the cottage. Occasionally carts could be heard and the odd groan as a heavy weight was lifted from the beach. She had been warned to pay no heed to them. They knew it was smugglers but the rule was that those who saw nought could tell no lies.

'Please, allow me.' Zachariah bent over by her side and calmly took over making up the bed.

'I can make my own bed, Mr Rudd,' Annie said, somewhat ungraciously.

'I'm glad to hear it.' He smiled at her. 'But this one will be mine. I have no wish to infringe on your hospitality any more than I need to.' He then took out a couple of coins from his pocket and offered them to her. 'I think this should cover it.'

Annie could see as they lay in his large open hand that there was enough money there to pay Nellie for two weeks' rent. Despite herself, Annie's face coloured. She had never taken money from a stranger before, and hated the idea they were in need of it now.

'You shall have to sort that out with my father, sir.'

Annie was about to step away when her father limped in through the doorway. He quickly closed the door against the driving sand and icy wind that accompanied him in. He looked at them standing by the palette together, Annie's face flushed and Zachariah still holding out the coins to her.

'I was just offering Miss Darton my rent money, sir.' He placed the coins on the table and sat down on the bed to finish his drink.

Her father looked at the coins as Annie pulled out a chair for him then fetched his tea.

'You are very generous, sir, unless, that is, you are to be staying here for a month.' Samuel's voice was pleasant, but Annie sensed he was not completely at ease. Normally relaxed, Annie wondered if it was the news of Ned King's murder that had upset him, or their unwanted tenant.

'Not at all, Mr Darton.' Zachariah smiled genially. 'I am just grateful to have a warm bed. Have they caught the murderer of the lighthouse keeper?'

Annie cringed, because that was how

she still thought of her father.

'No, not yet. The news is just breaking, and the yeomanry are just starting to go through the hamlet asking questions. No doubt they'll be sniffing around here by mornin'. I saw you at the church, didn't I?'

'Yes,' Zach answered.

'Did you know Seth?' Samuel asked, as he rubbed his bad leg and sipped his hot tea.

'Seth?'

'The man whose funeral it was,' Samuel explained.

'No.' Zachariah stood up. 'If you'll excuse me I shall walk into the hamlet. I'll be back before dark.' He nodded politely to them both and left.

Annie flinched from the draught as the door shut, then turned around to her father.

'Well, Father?' she asked.

'Well, what, daughter?' he replied.

'What happened to Ned King and who and what is our paying guest?'

Samuel stood up, stretched and said

nonchalantly, 'I don't know.'

'Don't know to which question?' Annie persisted.

'Either and all, Annie. Nothing is clear.'

He picked up his stick and walked to the door.

'Where are you going, Father?' Annie asked as he put his hand on the wooden latch.

'To find out some answers, lass.'

Annie put her hand on his arm.

'It's cold and dangerous. There is a murderer on the loose and we don't know who the stranger is.'

'And I'm your father and it is I who should tell you of the dangers, not you me.' He kissed her forehead. 'Now be a good daughter and have my dinner ready before I return, and don't fuss.'

Annie was left as one more blast of salty sea air entered the cottage, and her father, limping, and already tired, left.

4

Annie set about her task of gutting her fish. She slipped the sharp knife furiously into the belly nearly ruining her job. Her mind was filled with indignation at being left by the hearth like a . . . a woman! She was one, but Annie felt life had offered her more than the normal rôle of her sex.

She had helped her father tend the light, even venturing out in a cobble to help save lives. She was just as at home on the sea in one of the local flat-bottomed crafts as most fishermen, yet what was she now?

Annie stared down at the guts she had just removed from the cod in front of her, and spoke quietly. 'A daughter who's needed to keep house for her crippled father.'

She didn't know whom she felt more frustration for, herself or Samuel. Both would prefer their old life, neither had any choice over their new one.

Annie rebuked herself for being such a misery and set about laying the table for three. How odd it seemed to her because there had just been the two of them for so long. She felt uneasy as she imagined the stilted conversation to come. Then she smiled. One night, then he, her mysterious stranger, would be gone. Her thoughts returned to Ned King.

If the yeomanry heard about Amos's threats, would they arrest him, she wondered. Although the lad had spoken rashly at his father's funeral, Annie did not think for one moment he would kill him — well, not in such a dramatic manner. But who would? She prayed her father would return home soon. It was no time for a lame man to be wandering around in the dark.

There was a frantic knock on the door. Annie rushed over to it and could hear Nellie's voice shouting at the other side.

'Open that door, Annie.' The hoarse voice was shouting her words as they were taken away by the wind.

Annie unlatched it and instantly it was swung wide as Nellie's short figure entered, closely followed by Zachariah, carrying her father.

'Put him on his bed.'

Nellie pulled Annie back by the arm until Samuel was laid on his palette.

'What happened?' Annie removed her father's damp coat with the help of Nellie whilst Zachariah pulled off her father's boots. He looked pale, grey almost, and his skin had an unhealthy sheen.

'He collapsed by the inn,' Zachariah answered. His voice seemed to show genuine concern, but Annie couldn't help being angry with him. Since he had appeared, a man had been murdered and now her father lay ill. Was he connected with any of these events, Annie wondered.

Maude entered, her cloth cap almost lifting off her head, caught by the wind as she ran in.

'I have it, Nell,' she announced, her manner flustered as ever.

'Then give it to me, afore you drops it.'

Maude grabbed the small bottle from Nellie's hand and took it to Samuel. Annie had wrapped him in as many blankets as she could to bring him warmth again. He seemed cold to the touch but he had moaned and groaned as she and Zachariah between them removed his wet clothing. Annie did not like the stranger being so intimate with her father, particularly as he lay there, vulnerable and defenceless, but she needed Rudd's muscle. He had manoeuvred Samuel's limp body as if he were only a child.

Obviously, Annie thought, he was no stranger to hard work, even if something about his manner set him above an ordinary sailor or fisherman.

'What is that you're giving him?' Zachariah asked.

'Tonic. It'll make him strong again.'

Maude put the bottle to Samuel's lips. Annie watched, knowing that the old woman was wise in these things.

'Shouldn't we fetch the doctor?' Zachariah asked.

'And what good'll that do, lad?'

Maude's eyes widened as Nellie rounded, hand defiantly on her hip.

'I just thought the man needs a proper doctor to diagnose his illness. Doesn't Dr Harpham still practise in the town?'

Zachariah flushed slightly as the three women's attention was taken from Samuel and focussed inquiringly on him.

'Dr Harpham moved eight years ago. He established an infirmary over Gorebeck way, where he can practise all he likes.' Maude chuckled at her play on words, then snapped, 'You could always drag Dr Warren out of the inn but you'd have to drag him through a few waves to sober him up first!'

'There isn't any hospital around these parts then?' Zachariah persisted.

He showed no sign of being cow-towed by Nellie's brusque manner. Annie suspected he was used to fishermen's wives, and worse.

'Oh, aye, lad, there is.'

Maude took the bottle of elixir from Nellie and gave it to Annie whose eyes were fixed on the sleeping figure in front of her. She heard the banter around her but the only thing she took in was that the stranger obviously was familiar with the town, or at least he used to be.

'Then why don't I take him there tomorrow?' he offered.

'No!' Annie almost shouted out the word in her panic. 'Not the hospital, never!'

Nellie's laugh almost became a cackle. 'He's not goin' anywhere, lass. Don't yer fret.' Nellie stood square on to the stranger although her head was barely level with his chest. 'Mr Rudd, people don't go to Saint Bart's expecting to get better. They're sent to breathe their last, and when they have, old Blenkinsop sells the bodies to the surgeons over York way. He's not goin' anywhere. He just needs his rest in a good Christian home.'

Annie had had enough. 'I think you're correct, Nellie. Father needs to rest and keep warm. Perhaps in the morning he'll be his old self again.' She moved confidently over to the door.

Nellie, closely followed by Maude, bid Annie good-night.

'Annie, if he gets any worse send him for us.' Nellie gestured with her thumb towards Zachariah.

Annie thanked them and was touched by the way Nellie, hard as she was, had looked out for them since they had been forced out of the lighthouse.

Once they had gone, Annie, who was feeling emotionally drained by this long and most unusual day, looked to her father, who slept soundly, and then to her guest.

'Would you like something to eat?'

He stood instantly and looked amidst the pots on the hearth.

'You sit by your father if you wish. I'll get something for the both of us.'

Annie started to protest but he merely pulled a chair halfway between the fire and her father's bed and gestured for her to sit down. Before she had time to protest further she found herself presented with a fork and a pewter platter on which her food was served.

'Eat it. You may not feel as though you want to, Miss Darton, but you need your strength and rest, too.'

He smiled down at her and she could not help but look gratefully back at him. Annie stared at the tall figure in front of her and, without any sensation of fear of him, asked, 'Who or what are you, Mr Zachariah Rudd?'

He sighed and turned away to serve his own food.

'Miss Darton, I should like to answer your question earnestly, but please allow me the right to defer that answer until tomorrow. Then I will have spoken to Benedict and had some long-sought answers myself.'

Annie smiled politely.

'Then I shall await your reply with interest. I suggest, though, that you conclude your business sooner rather than later if the yeomanry are going to question everyone in the hamlet.'

Zachariah nodded and they ate in silence, Annie wondering what tomorrow would in fact bring, and prayed that her father would awaken, and be able to see it.

Annie dressed as light was just breaking. She washed her face in the bowl of cold water, which she always placed each night on the small table in the corner of her open loft room. She quickly brushed her voluminous hair and put on her cap to try to restrain it. Then, after quickly fastening her apron, she pulled on her black boots and climbed down the ladder. She hadn't meant to rise even as late as this, but she had sat with her father for so long the night before that she had had little enough sleep as it was.

'Good morning, Miss Darton.' Zachariah's voice almost caused her to miss the last step of the ladder. She turned with some embarrassment to face him. Annie had forgotten about their unwanted guest and she had climbed down the ladder in her normal carefree manner, not thinking that she may have someone watching her.

Annie nodded politely.

'Good morning, Mr Rudd. You are awake early.'

He was dressed in finer clothes than those of the night before. His jacket was not new but it was of good-quality wool. The buttons shone as if buffed with a military precision and, against his black trousers, boots and neatly tied silk scarf, he had all the appearance of the gentry. Annie quickly turned her attention from the mysterious, yet handsome, stranger to her father who was sitting propped up against his pillows drinking a cup of warm broth.

'Father.' She bent down and kissed his cheek. 'I should . . . '

'You should have slept in longer, Annie.' He smiled at her then sipped his broth slowly and carefully. 'I am not a child that I need my daughter to become as my mother, and sit fretting at my bedside. Robert here made me a fine drink.' He lifted his hand up slightly as he spoke.

'Zachariah, Father,' Annie corrected him gently and looked at the two men exchanging glances. Zachariah turned away as she caught his eye.

'Hmm, oh, yes, Zach. Well, he made me a fine broth and that is what I'll be — just fine in no time.' He gave Annie the small bowl that was only half-emptied. Then he rested and closed his eyes again. Annie was glad that he was conscious but he was obviously confused and weak.

'I have to go out now, Miss Darton. I expect to be back for my bag after I have been to the hall. Thank you for your hospitality. I'm sure your father will recover with your loving care. Is there no decent doctor left around these parts?'

'I think there is, possibly within a day's travel. I have an aunt who may be able to offer some help. I shall go to see her later, if Nellie or Maude will watch over him for me.' Annie tried to sound optimistic but spoke in a lowered voice. If Samuel knew she intended to ask her Aunt Amelia for help he would have another turn.

The truth was, though, that she felt they had little alternative. Work for men was scarce enough. The local women and children already filled the jobs, which were traditionally theirs in this tight-knit fishing community. Strangers were not welcomed or encouraged.

Annie and Samuel had been respected whilst working the light, but of course then they were at a safe distance. With the murder and the local yeomanry sniffing around, they would close ranks even more. No, she couldn't work and look after her father so she would have to appeal to the Christian duty of his sister, Amelia, and her wealthy, if not miserly mine-owner husband, Mr Ruben Horatio Hammond.

'I shall be back before nightfall.' He walked over to the door. 'Miss Darton . . . '

Annie looked at Zachariah as he hesitated by the door. 'Yes, Mr Rudd?'

'When you venture out, take care. If you need help, please remember I shall be at the hall.'

'Thank you, Mr Rudd, I shall.'

Annie watched him go. How strange, she thought. He talked like he had some sort of authority, yet looking at the well-worn bag he had left there with what would appear to have been his worldly possessions, you would have thought he was just another sailor, desperately seeking work.

Annie stared at the bag. She was tempted to see what was inside it. She picked it up and found it was quite heavy.

'Out of sight, out of mind,' she said quietly and opened a cupboard that was built on to the stone wall of the cottage. She pulled out a few plates and a pan, then removed the false back to it, revealing a storage space large enough to take a bale of silk. She rolled the bag in and replaced the panel, leaving the cupboard as it was.

She had not given in to temptation but, if Nellie and Maude were left here they would, of that she was certain. She wasn't sure why she should protect the stranger from their prying eyes. Part of her thought the two old biddies knew too much about everyone's business anyway. Annie's instinct told her that, no matter what Zachariah was, he meant them no harm.

Samuel was sleeping soundly — too soundly in Annie's opinion.

'Father, Father,' she repeated but did not shake him. Now would be a good time for her to see if Nellie was up. If she was, then Annie could make her way to Hammond Hall. Annie always grinned when she thought of its name. It was a large house, but her aunt had renamed it Hammond Hall when they had bought the old place for a knockdown price some years ago. It had been home to the local wagon-maker's family for years until drink and gambling took over his soul, landing him in jail with the other bankrupts.

Annie had wrapped herself in her cloak, when there was a loud knocking on her door. She quickly opened it as she did not want her father to be disturbed at all.

'Good morning, sir,' Annie greeted the captain of the local yeomanry.

The cape of his coat was lifting in the wind, nearly displacing his hat.

'May I come in, ma'am?' The man promptly stepped inside without awaiting an answer. One guard stayed at the door, another followed him in. Annie quickly shut it behind them.

'Now you are in, I must ask you to speak quietly. My father is a sick man and needs his rest.'

Annie gestured to her father who breathed shallowly and slept still.

The captain nodded but his eyes were everywhere. Annie could not understand why, but she was pleased that Mr Rudd's bag was well hidden. No matter what it contained she would feel ill-at-ease should these men search it. Besides, how could she explain they were innocent if it contained contraband or anything untoward?

'Is anyone else here?' the captain asked.

'No, we are on our own.' Annie watched as the soldier climbed her ladder and disappeared into her space.

'Who sleeps here?' The captain pointed to Zachariah's palette.

'I shall if my father takes a turn worse than he already has,' Annie answered as honestly as she could. She did not care for the man's manner.

The soldier returned and opened the cupboard, moving the plates and pan. Satisfied, he closed the door and probed under both beds with his bayonet.

'What do you know about Ned King

and the lighthouse?' the captain asked her curtly.

'Nothing and a lot.' Annie watched the captain's face as he walked over to her. He stood a head above her and looked down his long nose in a patronising manner.

'Explain yourself, miss,' he said and gently stroked her cheek with his gloved finger. She stepped back.

'I know nothing of Ned King but my father used to be keeper of the Gannet Rock Light,' Annie explained proudly.

The captain tilted his head on one side staring intently at her.

''Tis a shame then that he is so ill. We are in need of his knowledge. As soon as he wakes, send word and I shall have my man at the light to speak to him.' He took a step towards her again. Annie's face flushed. She did not like the game he played. She was not a village harlot. She could tell him all he needed to know about the light, but his type saw her as a woman only. It would not occur to him to ask her to go and help the soldiers man it by explaining what needed to be done.

'You are not like the common fishermen's women, miss.' He bent his head so that he could whisper into her ear. Moving the bonnet and her hair with his finger he spoke softly. 'You almost sound educated. I shall remember you.' He glanced at her father before continuing. 'I could make your father's bed a more comfortable one, if you make mine a more pleasurable one.' His cold moist lips glanced a kiss on her cheek. She backed away and was about to unleash a barrage of rebuke when Nellie opened the cottage door.

'Ah, Captain Lorcan, there yer be,' Nellie exclaimed and winked discreetly at Annie before his gaze left her.

'Who is looking for me and why?' The captain gestured for his soldier to leave as he looked at Nellie's short figure, dressed in ragged hat and bonnet, her skin never washed, grimy with years of exposure to salty sea air.

She smiled broadly, revealing her few teeth.

'Why me, of course, Nellie, sir. I heard how yer men had a suspect held at the inn. Tell me, sir, will we be safe in our beds this night?'

The captain looked down upon Nellie as she stood next to the open door.

'You will be, I can guarantee that.' He half smiled at Annie, and touched his finger to his hat in an almost mocking salute. 'Think on my words, miss. I shall return. Until then, good day.'

5

Zachariah walked the two-and-a-half miles from the bay, up through the glen, sheltered by the twisted branches of the wind-blown trees. He alighted by the coastal road, which would lead him to the gates of the Sunnington Hall estate — his rightful home.

How he could begin to explain who he really was to Miss Annie Darton was beyond him, until he was able to find out precisely what had befallen his family after he had been so brutally abducted by a press gang.

Fifteen years had passed by. The boy he was, Robert Stockyard, was crushed by a régime of discipline that demanded constant work, hardship and loyalty to the Crown, for whom he had the pleasure of fighting for in HMS Navy. The boy, Robert, had demanded they released him and contact his father,

Squire Thomas Stockyard, to obtain his release. He was gentry, too young for the service and wrongfully abducted, but all he got for his pleas was a sound beating, a place on the deck of a ship to sleep, and worse, he was made to use the name Zachariah Rudd.

He prayed and waited for his father to find him. He never did, and Robert became Zachariah, realising he either had to adapt to his new life or die. He chose life and, with the occasional guidance of a young lieutenant, survived. The lieutenant became a captain and when they were stepped down after Bonaparte made an uneasy peace, they turned to the merchant sea life.

Young Zachariah found himself in the East Indies. He had dreamed of returning home, but with the war with France rekindled, many letters had remained unanswered.

The gravestone in the churchyard had told him one awful truth already and raised another sickening question in his mind. His mother was dead, but the reference to her murdered son, Robert, which was inscribed on the small headstone next to hers, had him transfixed until the beautiful Miss Darton stumbled across his path.

He placed his hand on the ornate iron gates and stared down the gravel-covered driveway to the grandeur of the hall beyond.

'This should feel like home, but it does not. Mother is dead. Father is . . . where? Why is Benedict, the heir, here and what of Uncle Hughe?'

Zachariah shook his head as he started walking down the strangely familiar drive to his old home.

He knocked hard on the door with the large brass lion. It looked somehow neglected. In his young days the household kept everything in impeccable order. Looking closer he could see that some rooms in this grand old building had been shut up. Then he stepped back and looked up at the windows to the room where his father had always slept. He thought he saw a figure but, if he did, it backed away quickly from view. Perhaps, he thought, it was a servant daydreaming instead of working.

A severe-looking servant, dressed all in black, opened the door.

'Yes?'

'I wish to speak to Squire Thomas Stockyard.'

Zachariah instantly disliked the pompous attitude of the man. No servant should patronise a visitor in such a manner. He had looked Zachariah up and down and then raised an eyebrow as he peered beyond him, as if looking for his horse or trap. At the mention of his father's name, though, the servant's attention returned immediately to Zachariah's face.

'The hall is now under the ownership of Squire Benedict Stockyard,' the man answered staring at Zachariah. 'Good day . . . sir.' He tried to shut the door but Zachariah was strong, determined and sufficiently annoyed with the man, that he pushed it open wide using

70

the flat of his boot.

The servant was flustered by his action.

'Have care, sir!'

'Oh, I care. I wish to see Squire Benedict.'

Zachariah was standing inside the hall on the marbled floor that he had played on so happily as a child.

'Who shall I say is calling, sir?' The servant gestured that he should sit on a chair at the side of the hallway and wait.

Zachariah stood firm.

'Tell him Robert wishes to speak with him.'

The servant nodded and left, swiftly. None of the portraits of his mother or father hung on the walls. His uncle's image stared out of a huge painting hung at the top of the first flight of stairs, covering the facing wall.

The servant returned from upstairs.

'Squire Stockyard is not able to see anyone this morning. He has only recently returned from a long trip.'

The supercilious servant opened the door.

Zachariah did not hesitate. 'His trip was not as long as mine has been, of that I can assure you.' Without further conversation he climbed the stairs three at a time and did not stop until he had flung open the door of what had always been his father's private room.

'What mean you by this intrusion?' The words were spluttered out of his cousin's mouth, almost slurred. The man looked as though he was recovering from a hangover. He had always been shorter and rounder than Robert and the difference between them had only been exaggerated by the years. Zachariah — Robert — had become strong, firm and tanned by his life, whereas the paunchy, spoiled cousin of his had grown into a pale and paunchier indulgent man.

'What in the devil's name do you think you are doing in a gentleman's bedchamber? I shall have you evicted immediately!' Benedict reached out towards the bell-pull but Zachariah stepped in front of him and smiled.

'Ben, don't you recognise me?' He stared at Benedict's face and saw a realisation cross him. His eyes appeared to sparkle as Robert told him who he was but then they clouded over angrily and the man turned away. 'It is me — Robert. Where are Father and Uncle, and what happened to my mother? I saw her grave in the church grounds. Why wasn't she buried on the estate?'

Benedict rounded on him.

'You, whoever you are, are a cad and a bounder and I shall not have you trying to blackmail me here with your fanciful stories.'

Zachariah could hear feet running up the stairs and along the landing towards them. Why was Benedict denying the truth? Had it been too much of a shock for him?

'You know who I am, you recognised me. I saw it in your eyes.'

Two burly men appeared in the

doorway, one carrying a pistol. The manservant stood tall behind them.

'Sir, does yer need any 'elp?' one of the men asked.

'Yes, Tilby. You can escort this man off my estate.' He looked from Tilby to Zachariah. 'Do not return here, ever! Robert, my dear cousin, was murdered fifteen years ago and is as dead as his long-suffering mother. Bless her soul. Now go before I have you arrested.'

'Vigilante et orate,' Zachariah added, before he left and saw the expression on his cousin's face darken further. *Watch and pray* had been a phrase used by the old vicar, Reverend O'Leary of the chapel on the estate and the town church. He, too, like the family doctor, had moved on.

Zachariah was marched to the gates and shoved beyond them. He watched in silent outrage as they were closed to him. All this should be his father's or his. Whatever had happened here? He had no idea, but somehow he would find out all of his answers and soon.

* ★ ★

Annie waited until her father regained consciousness from his deep sleep. She smiled at him with affection and great relief when he opened his eyes and spoke to her.

'Have you been there all night, lass?'

'No, but you have, and that's where you're staying. You need to rest. It was lucky for you that Zachariah brought you home or you would have frozen to death out there.'

He snorted but made no attempt to move. Annie knew instantly he was feeling really ill, because he would never lie around in bed longer than he needed to.

'Where's young Robert?' he asked Annie and looked around the small cottage.

Her heart felt heavy. He was obviously still confused. Annie decided this was no time for pride — she had to get him help and soon. She gave him a warm drink, which he sipped reticently, then she propped his head gently back on his pillow. How she wished it were a linen-covered duck-down pillow. Her mind returned to Aunt Amelia's house. He needed to be cared for there.

'Mr Rudd left early this morning. He had business with Sir Benedict Stockyard,' Annie answered. She did not want to worry or fluster him by correcting his mistake over Zachariah's name. It might only unsettle him if he were aware that his mind was in turmoil.

'I should think he has!' he exclaimed indignantly.

'What happened, Father?'

He smiled at her, but it was a tired smile.

'It's a long story. Robert will no doubt explain it to you when he comes back. He's sure to.'

Annie gave no thought to his reply. Her father had obviously misunderstood her question. His delirium was worrying, though.

'I meant what happened to you last

night? What did it feel like when you had your turn?'

'I slipped, and it hurt when I fell. What did you think it felt like?'

He did not look at her.

'Was it a chest pain or a dizziness of the head? Don't lie, I need to know.' Annie waited for his protest, objecting to her manner, but he didn't.

'I slipped,' he sighed, then added, 'after I went a bit dizzy — just a bit.'

'You need rest, Father.' Annie shivered. With the draught coming under the door, all heat from the fire seemed to be blown out. It was no good, Annie decided, she would have to visit Aunt Amelia and appeal to her charity. The thought sickened her, but now was no time for pride. Her father needed warmth, rest, care and good food. He could tell her off when his health was strong enough for his stubborn pride to return.

'Rest now.' Annie tucked him in, ignoring his groan of disapproval.

Annie waited for him to doze off

again and then went next door for Maude.

Nellie answered her knock.

'Well, Annie, how is the old goat?'

That was Nellie sounding caring, Annie thought.

'Weak, tired and ill.'

Nellie sniffed. 'He's made of strong stuff, girl, take heart.'

'I wondered if Maude would stay with him whilst I went to my Aunt Amelia's for help.'

Nellie laughed. 'You think Mrs Amelia of the hall will have her lowly brother in her home, when he's sickening with something?'

'He needs better care than I can give,' Annie answered honestly.

'Well, girl, what's wrong with me? I can look after the old fella. You get about yer business and I'll see that he's fine.' Nellie crooked her head on one side. 'Where's yer lodger then, or don't yer trust him?' Nellie asked.

'I don't even know the man,' Annie replied indignantly. 'He went out early,'

Annie explained, but said no more about where.

She hesitated slightly and Nellie raised her eyebrows and folded her arms. Annie had to take the offer gratefully and go quickly so that she could be back, hopefully with transport, to take her father up to the hall.

'Thank you, Nellie. I'll be as quick as I can.'

Annie wrapped her cloak around her and braced herself to walk along the soft, sandy beach, through Widow's Walk and up to the hall beyond the church. The sea's waves crashed against each other in the distance and she listened to the constant roar of their momentum as over and over she rehearsed what she would say to her aunt.

It took her the best part of half an hour to reach the ornate iron gates. The large, cobbled yard in front of the old house was once filled with three types of wagons, in various states of building and repair. Stables to either side of the yard had held the strongest horseflesh for the larger wagons. Now they had the family coach that took her uncle back and forth to his affluent mines, and a small buggy.

The house still looked dour and dark to Annie, but it suited her sombre uncle. Her aunt would have had it redecorated in the light styles of the large manors and true country houses, but that would have cost her uncle some of his profits. He made himself even richer, as he bled his workers dry. Annie was about to turn and go but an image of her father laying a-bed filled her mind and she had to open the gates and force herself to walk through them.

Before she reached the hall door, a butler opened it.

'Servant girls go to the back door!'

His voice was curt and Annie put her head high and answered him.

'Please tell the lady of the house her niece has called to see her on a matter of some family urgency.'

He looked her up and down, holding out his hand.

'Your calling card, miss?'

'I have no need of a card. Please tell Aunt Amelia that Miss Annie Darton wishes to see her urgently!' Annie stared at the man.

He turned, shutting the door behind him. Annie wrestled with her pride. She was doing this for her father, she told herself over and over.

The door opened again and she was ushered through to the morning-room. After a half hour had passed in which time she had not been offered anything to eat or drink, the door was opened wide.

'Well, my girl, I hope you have a good reason for bursting in here so early in the day, unannounced and demanding an audience with me!'

Her aunt's short and rather dumpy figure strutted past her and sat down on a two-seater settee by the window.

'Good morning, Aunt Amelia. I am so pleased to see you are looking so strong and healthy.'

Annie tried to be polite and remove all tone of sarcasm from her voice.

'I would say the same for you were it not for the rags you wear. My goodness, girl, you've walked half of Ebton sands into my house.'

She was staring at the trail of fine sand that had fallen from Annie.

Annie glanced down to see the hem of her dress and boots caked in fine damp sand.

'I do apologise. I was in such a hurry I didn't think.'

'Obviously not. So why were you in such a hurry to see me after all this time? Colonel Sanderson was asking after you only two weeks since. He is such a lonely old soul.' Her aunt arranged her skirts as she spoke, and Annie couldn't help but agree with her for once — he was an old soul.

'It's my father,' Annie started but her aunt interrupted her straight away.

'Obviously. What's the old fool done now?'

Her aunt folded her hands neatly on her lap and stared at her niece, who was still standing in the middle of the room.

'He took a fall.'

'Again! Does the man have a problem with drink, my girl?' Her aunt looked perplexed at the thought. 'Surely I'm not to have a drunkard in the family. Is it not bad enough to have a failed lighthouse keeper and cripple as a brother!'

'He is not a drunk and never has or will be! He is neither a failed light keeper nor a cripple. He had an accident and now cannot do the job he loved and was gifted at. At present he lays a-bed, he needs to see a doctor and have somewhere warm to sleep with good food to give him strength. As his sister and a Christian, I thought you might find it in your heart to offer him these things until he is strong again.' Annie sounded sharp. She had tried not to let the fury and frustration she was feeling escape from her, but she could not control the outrage at her aunt's hypocrisy.

'My dearest Annie, of course I care deeply about his and your well-being but you have forgotten one thing. The estate is my husband's, not mine.' Aunt Amelia sounded patronising.

'Perhaps you could persuade your husband to look kindly on your brother in his hour of need.' Annie stared back at her.

'Perhaps I could. We shall see. Firstly, I shall send for a doctor to see him. Should his illness be no more than an injury and not a contagion, then your uncle might allow you both to stay in the rooms to the back of the hall.'

'I ask merely that you take care of my father. I shall visit daily, but I would not put any extra burden on you or your husband.' Annie lifted her chin defiantly as she spoke. Why on earth had she come?

'Annie, dear, if I persuade your uncle to pay for your father's convalescence we would expect you to be here also.

After all, he would want you with him. A young lady cannot live on her own. What would people think? Secondly, you of course would be our guest also, and help me entertain your uncle's business associates.'

Annie wondered why she cared what people thought about her. What would they think if they knew about Zachariah sleeping at the cottage, too? Her aunt continued.

'No, my dear. If your father is fit enough to be brought here then you shall accompany him. My carpets would not take the amount of sand and dirt your visits would inflict upon them. Now go and I shall send a doctor forthwith. If there is no contagion then you shall both be welcome here tomorrow.'

Annie nodded. 'Thank you, Aunt Amelia.'

Annie walked to the door, which had been opened for her by the butler. As she was about to pass through it her aunt said, 'You will be just in time to join my husband, myself and the good colonel for dinner on Friday evening. They will both be delighted.'

Annie spun around and opened her mouth to speak, but her aunt lifted her hand.

'No, child, don't thank me. I am sure that your uncle will find it in his heart to pay for your father's recuperation, when he hears you will be staying with us once more.'

6

Annie went into the church and prayed. Firstly, for her father's health to improve, and secondly for the wisdom of what she had just done. She then wandered to her mother's grave and paused awhile, whilst trying to find comfort in her memories of the beautiful woman she had known for such a short time in her life. She read the words on the headstone when the voice in her mind was replaced by the deep voice of the stranger.

'Through the darkest storm,
And the tempest's height,
Guide us, dear Lord,
By Your kindly light.'

Annie turned and saw Zachariah standing behind her, looking deeply thoughtful at the headstone.

'That's beautiful,' he said.

'It was a prayer she made up. We

used to say it together each night when I was a child,' Annie explained with the heartfelt warmth that she had always experienced when her mother said those comforting words to her. She had never heard them spoken out loud for all those years.

'I take it this lady was your mother?' Zachariah asked.

'Yes.'

Annie was surprised when he cupped her elbow gently in his hand and guided her away.

'Come with me a moment and let me introduce you to mine.'

It was an overly familiar gesture for such a new acquaintance, particularly as they were alone, albeit in a churchyard, and yet it seemed so natural and unintrusive. He stopped by the grave where she had seen him crouched at the side of at Seth's funeral.

'My mother.'

He let go of her elbow and gestured to the large gravestone.

'But she was Lady Stockyard!' Annie gasped.

The Stockyard family was one of the wealthiest families around the Ebton area. She then read the name on the small gravestone at its side.

'Robert Francis Stockyard, beloved son, aged twelve, murdered. May he RIP.' She turned and looked at him. He seemed deeply troubled by her words.

'Father called you Robert. Why? Is he confused, or was he your brother? Does Father know something that I don't?' Annie asked.

'No, he is the only person around these parts who is not confused or misled. He actually sees clearly. Robert was not murdered; he was press-ganged, renamed Zachariah Rudd and taken on board an HMS frigate, to a place far from these shores. But now he has come back to find that his mother and his uncle are both dead! His father has disappeared, and his cousin . . . ' Zachariah clenched both of his fists and looked up at the sky, then cleared his throat. 'His cousin is refusing to acknowledge him. Benedict has taken over my birthright, and accused me of being an imposter!' He looked at Annie intensely. 'Who will believe me now?'

'I will,' Annie answered honestly, yet was surprised that she trusted this stranger with all her heart.

'What are you going to do, Zach . . . I mean, Robert?'

Annie was confused. She didn't know what to say to this man. What should she call him? Which was his chosen name? Annie suddenly felt quite in awe of this tall, handsome man. Here she was on her own, talking to the heir of a wealthy and titled man, Lord Thomas Stockyard. Yet he stood before her, vulnerable and disinherited.

'I will remain Zachariah. I don't doubt for one minute that if Benedict can have me thrown in prison, and pay to have the key lost, he would do just that. No, damn him! At the moment he has everything, and I, nothing.'

He turned to face the sea.

Annie moved next to him.

'No, he doesn't,' Annie said, surprising him with her simple and positive reply. 'He does not have the truth on his side, and you do.'

Zachariah laughed openly at her. Yet, she did not feel insulted for his laugh was not scornful but one of genuine humour. He placed his hand reassuringly on her shoulder.

'Oh, Miss Annie Darton, you honestly think that will make the slightest bit of difference to anyone?' He stared into her eyes earnestly and her heart felt warmed by the intimacy of their conversation.

Annie looked straight back into his deep, dark brown eyes and smiled confidently.

'Yes, I do. Where you have truth, then there must also be the proof to justify it. When you have the proof in your hands — justice will be yours.'

'Miss Annie Darton, forgive me for being so bold, but I am exceedingly glad that it is under your roof I have found a place to rest my head.'

He smiled at her and Annie had to fight an unusually brazen impulse to embrace him and rest her troubled head against his chest.

She had never felt as drawn to any man in her life as she did to her very own mysterious stranger. Anne smiled until she remembered that she was no longer to sleep under her own roof. What had she done?

'Zachariah, we must return to Father.' Annie turned towards the path through the churchyard. She dismissed her mad notions of desire for Zachariah as symptoms of the worry she carried over Samuel's health and concern for her new friend's predicament. At speed, she headed for Widow's Walk.

The tide was coming in and the sounds of breaking waves filled her head. She did not hear Zachariah run up alongside her until he spoke. She was leaning into the wind, when his now familiar voice asked after her father's well-being.

'I have an aunt who lives at Hammond Hall. She is by no means as wealthy as your own family but they are comfortable. I have asked her for help, although my father will be far from pleased at my intervention.'

Annie sighed and carried on walking with her head bent low.

'I am not aware of another hall so near here. Has it been built since I was . . . since I left?'

Annie grinned. 'Do you remember a wagon-makers near the church?'

'Well enough, yes. It was a dilapidated building with a cobbled yard.'

'Aunt Amelia and Uncle Thomas bought it cheaply, spent some money repairing the house, adding some stabling and renamed it Hammond Hall. He owns mines and they needed somewhere affordable that could give them a home befitting their acquired status.'

She laughed at the memory of her father's quips when he first heard about Amelia — or Pudding, as he called her, being the lady of the hall.

'New money,' Zachariah stated matter-of-factly.

'Blood money more like,' Annie answered. 'His mines are filled with poor women and children alongside the menfolk. They're worked like animals. It's criminal,' Annie snapped in her disgust.

'Then if your feelings are so strong against them, you must be very worried about your father to place yourself on their charity.'

Zachariah stopped and turned Annie to face him. The way his eyes seemed to reach into hers made her feel very strange inside. It was deeply personal, movingly honest and very intrusive.

'Annie Darton, I'll make you a promise and, God willing, I shall be able to keep it. Do what you must to secure a warm bed and medicine for your father now. Somehow, I shall secure the proof I need and be restored to my birthright. Then you will not need to fall on these people's charity. I shall see you both have decent living accommodation. I owe you that.'

'You owe us nothing. You hardly know us at all.'

Annie stood, battered by the wind and sea spray, yet oblivious to the cold as she gazed up at the handsome stranger who bent her mind and emotions into places they had never been before.

'Well, if I don't owe you, Miss Darton, I certainly am indebted to your father. If the old lighthouse keeper can recognise the boy who would sneak out of the estate to play on the beach, then he may hold the key to the truth. I need to talk to him now, before you are both beyond my reach. If he knows any of the truth of my past and what has happened since I left, then my search for proof must begin with him.'

He gently bent over and kissed her forehead as she stared up at him, wishing with all her heart she would never be beyond his reach.

The warm touch of his moist lips set

her senses alight, and shocked her into looking nervously around them. She thought she saw a figure disappearing into the dunes. Quickly she continued towards the cottage.

'Miss Darton, forgive me . . . I did not mean to be so forward. It is just that . . . '

Annie turned towards him, her back to the wind and kept walking.

'It really is all right, Mr Rudd. I understand, really I do. Your emotions are in turmoil. Please let us not mention it again.'

'I wish to never forget it, or you, Miss Darton.'

Annie rushed to the cottage door, not looking back at him again; however, she knew he still followed her. She could feel his presence and it sent shameful thoughts through her mind. What would it have felt like if his lips had lingered and caressed hers, and she had returned the kiss?

'You sure took yer time, Annie Darton. Don't yer know others have lives to live, too?' Nellie glared at her than nodded to Zachariah.

'Sorry, Nellie. I was held up,' Annie explained and blushed.

'Yes, I saw.' Nellie hobbled towards her own cottage door. 'Doctor's been. He said as how it's not a contagion but he needs good victuals and rest. They'll send summit from the house to collect you both.' She looked up at Zachariah and smiled broadly. 'Does you still need a place to sleep?'

'Yes, I do ma'am,' he answered politely.

Nellie laughed, exposing her discoloured teeth.

'Then you can keep her bed warm until she needs it again. For they'll not be welcome up at Pudding's place any longer than needs be.'

Nellie disappeared inside her cottage with her raucous laughter still audible outside.

Annie was too embarrassed to look at Zachariah or Nellie and slipped inside to see her father and tell him the news.

'Father, how do you feel?' Annie smiled her brightest most cheerful smile. She'd used the same one ever since she was a child — the overly innocent one that her father seemed to instantly suspect.

'Angry, furious, annoyed, murderous, should I continue?' He nodded to Zachariah. 'Did you put her up to this sheer lunacy?'

'What lunacy, sir?' Zachariah asked innocently.

'Father, Zachariah did not even know about Aunt Amelia. You need proper care and warmth. You fell because you were ill; you are not being fussed over because you merely tripped over; you had a fever and were delirious.'

Zachariah squatted next to Samuel.

'Sir, forgive me cutting in on your private row, but I need your help.'

Samuel sighed and looked at him. 'Well I'm glad somebody around here values my opinion.' He glared at Annie, as she packed up their few belongings.

'You know who I am, don't you? How, sir?'

Annie watched the desperate expression on Zachariah's, or Robert's face. She also saw her father's face soften with compassion.

'Don't you remember, sir? I showed you the lighthouse and you wanted to know all about it?' Samuel grinned at him.

'Yes, it had the power of more than thirteen thousand candles, a rotating shaft and was fixed with twenty-one parabolic reflectors on each side of the frame.'

Samuel laughed at him and then coughed.

'You always were a bright child, eager to learn.'

'What happened here? Why was I thought to be dead — murdered?' Zachariah asked.

'Because, Robert, some fisherman off Whitby way found your washed-up body on the shore early one morning. It was too much for your poor father to identify you. He went quite mad with grief, so your uncle identified you instead.' Samuel sighed. 'It was all over so quickly. Your poor mother died within months.'

'But Father was a strong, sober man. He wouldn't have gone under at such a task, no matter how hideous he found it. My mother was weak. Without him she would never have survived, God rest her soul. She was a timid person, often suffering from melancholy. Is my father dead, too?'

'No, lad, he's put away somewhere. God knows where, but after that your uncle became Lord of the Manor, so to speak.' Samuel stopped thoughtfully. 'So, if you're not dead, and you look a fine, healthy specimen to me, if you don't mind my sayin' so for a dead un, where, then, did you go?' Samuel put his head back on the pillow.

'I was press-ganged. I wrote when I could but no-one ever replied. Then I stopped and decided to work until I earned enough to escape my life at sea and return home. I expected to find my mother and father waiting, wondering what happened to their long-lost son. So where did my uncle go?'

There was a noise outside and Zachariah stood up. He looked down anxiously at Samuel. Annie knew how much he needed the information.

'Why, he was killed in a riding accident four years since.' Samuel coughed and slumped on to the pillow again.

The door opened and the lieutenant arrived with two men. One was the doctor and the other was Colonel Sanderson. Annie saw the scowl on the lieutenant's face as the colonel greeted her warmly.

'My dear Miss Darton, I am so pleased to be able to offer a personal escort for you and your father. These are dangerous times. There is a murderer loose among us, we need to take care.' He glanced around the sparse cottage and shook his head. 'My dear girl, you deserve so much more than this.' His words were spoken softly to her.

Two soldiers lifted her father bodily. Samuel looked as though he was speaking to Annie, but Zachariah was in his line of vision.

'I should see Dr Harpham.'

'Dr Harpham left us to go to Gorebeck to open his infirmary,' Annie added quickly, as if offering her father solace. She saw Zachariah nod slightly.

'Who might you be?' The lieutenant turned his attention to Zachariah.

'Please let me introduce you,' Annie said brightly, addressing the colonel. 'This is an old friend of my father's. He will be renting the cottage whilst my father recuperates. It is a great relief to us to know our humble home will be cared for.'

The colonel looked sympathetically at her.

'My dear child, you need have no concerns over that, I assure you.'

As she was escorted to the door she turned to Zachariah.

'Please, make yourself at home. You should find all you need in the cupboard. Ask Nellie if you can't find anything.'

Zach nodded and she hoped he understood because his bag was still hidden in the secret compartment at the back of the cupboard.

7

Zachariah scratched his head. Events were not unfolding as he had planned. By now he should have been celebrating with his family by the large, open fire of his childhood, not hiding in a poky, little cottage that opened its door out on to the wide, sandy bay and a cold, unyielding sea. Where he once had a bedroom with a view that looked out over the estate to the moors beyond, he now had sand dunes and storms in its place.

Now even Miss Annie Darton had gone. He had seen many women and courted a fair few, but none of them had attracted him in the way she had. His feelings towards her were of an instant attraction for her character as much as her natural beauty. She had an inner grace about her that he found very pleasing and, despite her social rank, he found her charming. Unlike his mother who would take to her bed at the slightest whim, Annie was strong, determined and natural. She was happy to be as God had made her.

He opened the cupboard and moved the contents around. There was nothing there other than a few pots and pans. What could Annie have meant? He pushed the back of it but the wood held fast.

'Can I be of some assistance, sir?' Nellie's sharp voice took him by surprise.

'I was just seeing what was in here. Miss Darton told me to make myself at home.' He shut the cupboard door and stood up. Nellie closed the cottage door behind her.

Nellie chuckled. 'I bet she did.' She warmed her hands by the fire. 'You'd never convince those troops, yer know. Stand aside.'

Nellie opened the cupboard and sank to her knees. Zachariah watched her as her tiny, raggedy figure almost disappeared inside it. She grunted and groaned then, with a tug, she backed out dragging his bag with her. Then she quickly rearranged something in the cupboard and closed it up once more. She propped herself on one knee whilst she used a chair to pull herself back up. Zachariah offered to help her up.

'Get away with yer. I'm not that crabby yet!' Nellie grinned as she put both her hands on her bony hips. 'Well, is that what yer be lookin' for?'

'Yes, Nellie, but how did you know where it was?' Zachariah asked as he glanced inside the bag, checking the contents.

'Now, lad, I'm no thief of honest men. Yer are honest, aren't yer?' she asked with her head tilted on one side.

'I am but not many around seem to be,' Zachariah said and winked at her cheekily.

Nellie pulled out her pipe from her skirt pocket and sat down in Samuel's favourite chair by the fire.

'Well, you can trust old Nellie, so tell

us what it is yer need to know, lad.'

Just then the door opened and Maude came bustling in. She closed out the draught behind her and huddled next to Nellie by the fire. Nellie nodded at Maude.

'Don't worry about Maudie. She may look like she's got a few grains short of a beach, but she's safe as houses, aren't yer?'

Maude smiled and nodded her head eagerly, her tattered cloth bonnet looked in danger of falling off her head.

'I want to know what happened up at the hall?' Zachariah pulled up one of the other chairs and joined them.

'Well, Mrs Amelia said as she would take in Annie's father if she were nice to the colonel, I think, reading between the lines like. I mean, no-one else would warrant gettin' a colonel down here unless of course they found the murderer. Annie's a good lass but he has always hankered after her.'

Maude shook her head disapprovingly.

'I think it's disgustin'. He's old enough to be her father and besides, it's not fittin'. He should chase some town girl and leave young Annie alone.'

It was information that Zachariah had not expected. He was annoyed that he was in no position to help the young woman and her father. He knew Sanderson's type. They wanted to possess what they could not have. After living lives where they always got what they wanted, almost too easily, girls like Annie, who resisted, provided a challenge, like a stubborn fox in a hunt. Ultimately the fox died, though, from exhaustion and the hunter went for the next one, thirsty for new blood.

Somehow he had to solve his own problem and then help to untangle Annie from hers.

'That wasn't the hall you was enquiring about, though, was it, eh?'

Nellie looked pointedly at Zachariah who met her eyes and they stared at each other silently for a moment.

'No, it wasn't. I was referring to

Sunnington Hall.'

Zachariah had met Samuel on a few occasions, but was never seen in town because he had been cosseted up in the hall and grounds. He was never allowed to mix with the common townspeople, as his mother feared he would catch some incurable illness from them.

It was his uncle who had come to help him. He had seen the boy, Robert, climbing out of a window. It was Uncle Hughe who had covered for him whilst he explored the lighthouse. His uncle had said that no-one from town would see him so it would be safe. It was there that he was going when he disappeared — ambushed by the press-gang.

His uncle was the only one who could have directed the search in the correct place to look. Samuel did not know he was coming to see him again so the old man had no part in it. Because Robert never knew when the opportunity to escape on an adventure would arise, Samuel could not have either. It was his uncle who could have engineered the whole thing — his own father's younger brother. The revelation made his anger rise, and he stared intently at the small fire.

'What business is it you have with the Stockyards, man?' Nellie asked.

'I need to know what happened to Benedict's aunt and uncle. I know the aunt died, but what of her husband, Lord Thomas?'

'They said the old boy went mad. I thinks not. I heard he went screaming into the coach until they muffled him. His screams weren't of a madman but of a bloody furious one.' Nellie laughed.

Zachariah stared at her, and she cleared her throat and then sucked at her pipe before continuing.

'When he went, Dr Harpham went with him.'

Nellie made a clucking sound with her teeth.

'Funny thing was, Harpham had a big family like. He weren't that well off. Yet, suddenly he can up and move to Gorebeck and run his own place.

Funny how a man's fate can change, eh?' Nellie giggled.

Maude gave a start as a loud knock on the door was followed by it being flung open wide to reveal the figure of the lieutenant and two soldiers.

'What meaning do you have by this intrusion?' Zachariah stood up, almost knocking over the chair he had been sitting on.

'I, sir, am investigating a murder, and you . . . sir,' the lieutenant said as he looked him up and down, 'are a stranger to these parts and have no alibi for the time of the murder. No-one knows who you are or where you were. So you are being taken for questioning.'

Zachariah was about to launch into an attack when Maude stood up also and rushed to the lieutenant.

'But you're mistaken, sir.' She bobbed him a curtsey. 'I know who he is. Mr Zachariah Rudd, and he was with us, wasn't he, Nellie?'

She turned around and Nellie, who was still sitting, sucking her pipe said,

'Yes, he was that. We can both vouch for him and also the colonel's friend, Miss Darton, can. You can find them together at the new hall, sir.'

The lieutenant picked up Zachariah's bag and roughly emptied the contents all over the table.

'I protest!' Zachariah said and looked down at his belongings, noticing his pistol was not there, neither was a leather wallet and purse. He glanced at Nellie, who merely looked away.

The lieutenant left the items strewn over the table and floor.

'You, sir, will be watched and the first sign of suspicion I have, you will be arrested.'

Zachariah had no time to reply. The man left and Zachariah stared at Nellie.

'What did you do with my things?'

'How do yer know it weren't Miss Annie what done summit with yer things?' Nellie answered defiantly then sucked on her pipe and grinned to herself.

'Because I doubt she would think to.

Once hidden in there she would see no need to remove anything,' Zachariah answered.

' 'aven't yer forgotten yer manners, man? We've just stopped yer from bein' arrested.' Nellie looked up at him, raising both her eyebrows.

'Thank you, ladies.' He made a grand bowing gesture, then added, 'So what did you do with my things?'

Nellie rustled around in the ample tattered skirt of her dress.

'Here, it's all there so don't go getting insultin' and count it.' She handed him over the wallet and coin purse, then produced the pistol from the other side of her skirts. 'Them's dangerous. Yer should take more care, lad.'

'Thank you. I need a horse. It is vitally important that I go to Gorebeck immediately.' He packed up his belongings, but took his money and pistol with him. 'Will you put these things into the cupboard again?' He tossed Nellie a coin, which she caught and quickly pocketed.

'Who are you to them at the house?' Nellie asked.

Zachariah was grateful to the two old women but he did not trust them one jot. He suspected they had helped him as much for profit and out of habit; the locals loathed the authorities and were always trying to outwit them and the revenue men.

'If my business is completed and successful then you shall find out soon enough,' he said and opened the door. 'Now where could I rent a good horse, a swift one?'

Nellie strutted over to him.

'You can't, I can, Stockyard. For there is nought around here Nellie don't know about.' She had hissed the words quietly as she passed him and stepped outside.

'Then who killed your man at the lighthouse?' Zachariah asked quietly.

'That, ma boy, is summit you don't need to know. Them that does keeps their mouths firm shut. I suggest yer keep yer ears that way, too. Now follow me, milord. Oh, and he weren't my man.'

Nellie took him to the back of the inn. A large, burly man opened the door after Nellie gave two sharp knocks followed by a gap then one small one.

'Jake, he needs to borrow yer prancer, urgent like.' Nellie was craning her neck, looking up at the huge figure with a scar across his left cheek.

'What fer?' the man asked gruffly.

'Business, I'll vouch for him.'

Nellie looked him straight in the eye and winked.

'How long for?' The man was glaring at Zachariah but he stared back at him.

'A day, possibly overnight.' Zachariah was unsure.

Nellie pulled at the man's waistcoat until he bent low so that she could whisper something into the man's ear.

The man smiled broadly.

'Go on, Nellie. Yer take him, I'm busy.' With that the man shut the door.

'Come.' Zachariah followed Nellie to

a ramshackle hut behind the chapel. There a horse was stabled. At first sight it looked a poor specimen, but when he led it out into the open light he could see it was a fine animal with a raggedy cloth over its back and mud on its mane.

'Bring it back safe, or yer'll be a dead man.'

Nellie stepped nervously back from the animal as he saddled it.

Zachariah mounted it and answered, 'If I don't bring it back then there's a good chance that I will be a dead man!'

Maude had run up behind them and, as Zachariah rode the animal along the coastal path, she sighed, 'So handsome.'

Nellie looked at her and doubled in a fit of laughter, but Maude just stared at the rider until he was beyond her sight.

8

Annie tried hard not to have any eye contact with her father all the way to Hammond Hall. She could sense the tension in him as the coach rattled over the cobbled streets to Ebton and then was hauled up the bank from the coast road down to the bay.

She looked longingly at the sea before it was out of sight again, and to the light, forever standing out against the rocks and sea. Her feelings were in turmoil. She knew that her father desperately needed care, yet was worried that the short but tense journey would be too much for him, not to mention Aunt Amelia's no doubt smug forbearance of them.

Then there was the colonel whose eyes had not wandered from Annie since they entered the carriage. What was he to Amelia? Why was he so taken by her when he could buy a York lady, with his rank and money? Age meant nothing if a good match could be made amongst the gentry — new or old money, was still good money to them. Annie saw herself as plain and practical. She had no notion of her real value and beauty.

When they passed through the gates of Hammond Hall and over the rickety, cobbled stones, it was as if a dismal cloud settled over her.

'It won't be for long,' she whispered into her father's ear as two soldiers made ready to carry him into the hall. He grunted. Dr Bevin followed, issuing instructions to take good care of his charge. It was amazing what diligence money could buy, Annie thought.

'Allow me, Miss Annie.'

The colonel stepped down from the carriage and turned to help Annie. Instead of offering her his hand he held her waist firmly at either side and half lifted her out, smiling at her in a manner that made her deeply uneasy.

'Now, Annie, my dear, you no longer need to worry about the care of your father. I shall see he has the best, so you can think of yourself and your future more carefully in the days ahead. Give no more thought to that draughty old hovel. From this day forth you need only sleep in feather beds.'

Annie did not know what to say and for once was pleased to see her aunt blustering towards her.

'Oh, Colonel, how kind of you to come. My brother, he's . . . ' Amelia seemed at a loss for words.

'He's in need of our help, my dear kind Mrs Hammond. We shall see that he has the best, won't we?' The colonel's words were like a command and Amelia appeared only too happy to obey them.

'Well, of course, which is precisely why I sent for the good doctor and insisted he be brought to us, with our poor dear niece.' She linked arms with Annie and Annie felt her cringe as the lace of her dress touched her own apron. 'We will send for some more suitable attire, my dear, forthwith.'

'How did you know we were coming here, Colonel, if my aunt had not informed you?' Annie asked, as it was obvious that from her aunt's manner she had been as surprised as Annie was by the colonel arriving with his coach.

'I was with Dr Bevin when he received your aunt's request.' The colonel glanced at Amelia who flushed slightly, and Annie wondered what the wording had been of the request. No doubt along the lines of, 'If my brother has a contagion, lead him far away from me.'

'That was indeed a fortunate coincidence, Colonel. I thank you for your care and consideration,' Annie replied genuinely. 'Now if you would allow me, I should like to see my father is settled in comfortably.'

'Well, of course, child. Now I shall have Betty fetch you water and some clean clothes, then we must all take tea together.'

Aunt Amelia walked Annie into the hall as she summoned Betty, giving her instructions to have the guest room made up for Annie.

'But, milady, I thought you said we was to put her in the . . . '

'Betty! Did you hear my orders or not?' Amelia snapped at the hapless girl.

Betty paled and curtseyed quickly.

'No, ma'am, I mean, yes, ma'am, the guest room. This way, miss, if you please.' The maid quickly escorted Annie away from her aunt.

The colonel made his apologies but only after telling her aunt he should be glad to return for dinner, which she said she thought was a wonderful idea.

The apologetic maid opened the door to a cold guest room.

'I'm sorry, miss, I'll make up a fire straightaway. I'm sure your aunt mentioned a different room. I don't make mistakes, miss, not often, like.'

'I'm sure you were correct, but obviously this time Aunt Amelia did.'

Annie looked around and saw there was another door on the opposite side of the room.

'Where does that door lead to?' Annie asked.

'Oh, that used to be the master bedroom and this would be for the mistress of the house.' Betty started to clear the grate.

'Is that where my father will be?' Annie asked, thinking how convenient it would be if he were there.

'No, miss. Your father is in one of the cosy back rooms. Actually he will be better off there because they can be kept warm easy and they're near the servants' stairs should he be in need of owt. That's used as another guest room. Master Hammond says there's no good wasting money heating up two big rooms so he and the mistress sleep in the smaller rooms, too.'

'Betty, you do what you need to here and I'll sit with my father. Tell me when the water is ready and the room's above freezing.'

Annie smiled and left the maid frantically making the unused room habitable. It was bigger than Annie was used to, and in fact she would have preferred a cosy backroom.

Annie knew what Amelia's temper was like when she did not get her own way. She followed the sound of men's voices to the back landing, thinking that would lead her to her father's bedroom. Instead she realised she was listening to the colonel and the butler on the back stairs. Annie stopped before she reached them and tried to strain to hear what they were saying.

'I saw Tilby, sir,' the butler was whispering.

'Does Fletcher know?' Colonel Sanderson's voice was slightly clearer.

'No, sir, but Vickers is an angry man and he don't want any strangers coming back from the dead, so to speak.'

'Then we won't have to upset him, will we?'

Annie drew in her breath. Were they talking about Zachariah — Robert?

How could she warn him if they were? They had spoken in conspiratorial tones.

'See to it!' Colonel Sanderson said sharply.

'Yes, sir.'

Annie heard the sound of feet running back down the servants' stairs. She backed away from the stairwell and then walked briskly past the top as if she had just come from her room. The colonel appeared at the top as she crossed.

'Oh, Colonel, I thought you had left.' Annie gave a startled look and placed her hand to her chest.

'I do apologise, my dear. I merely remembered I needed to see Dr Bevin before I leave.'

Annie entered the room and the doctor and the colonel left. She looked at her father lying clean and comfortable in a bed with freshly-laundered linen sheets. She could not help but smile and knew as she sat on the comfy chair between the warm fire and his bed that she had made the correct decision, at least for her father.

'You look better already,' she said softly.

'Good! Then fetch me my clothes, coat and stick and I'll be out of this place before dinner.' He grumbled but, at the same time, nestled down on the soft bed.

'Pride comes before a fall, Father.'

'Don't talk to me about falling, girl!' He looked at her and half grinned. 'So how much of a fall are you prepared to take, hmm?'

'I don't know what you mean?' Annie shrugged her shoulders and stared at the flickering flames.'

'You look tired, lass.'

Annie glanced up at him in protest.

'That's the pot calling the kettle, isn't it?'

'Yes, you do. The colonel wants you, one way or another, Annie. Make sure you're wed before he has what he wants.' He winked at her and flushed slightly.

'I'll not marry unless it's for love.'
She still stared at the flames, thinking about what she'd heard. Did it refer to Zachariah Rudd? He had come back from the dead, hadn't he?

'Pride!'

Annie was deep in thought and hadn't realised her father was still staring at her.

'Well, what's it that's takin' up yer mind, Annie?' The flustered voice of Samuel took her by surprise.

'Nothing. Just silly thoughts, that's all,' Annie answered dismissively.

'Tell me, I'm not stupid and I know when there's summit up.'

Annie moved over and sat on the quilted bed cover.

'Father, tell me who Vickers is, please?'

'Jebidiah Vickers is a hard man. No-one knows much about him other than he runs the largest smuggling racket on our coast. He has Selwyn Fletcher and his local operation in the palm of his hand. Selwyn was a good man — of sorts. Looked out for the town and the locals, then Vickers spread his net wider and wanted a piece of the action here. At first Selwyn said no, but accidents started occurring — unexplained like. Fletcher realised he had no choice, or he'd have to start a fight, one that he couldn't win. Next thing, he finds out that Vickers is in deep with the London dealers.' Samuel started to sip some water.

'Dealers in what?' Annie asked.

'Oh, lass, this isn't stuff you should have in your head, girl.' He sighed and was reluctant to continue.

'Yes, it is, if I'm to help Robert regain his birthright.'

Samuel almost sat up but Annie stopped him.

'Careful, you have to rest.'

'Rest! You can't help the lad. He'll have to sort it out for himself. If he knows what's good for him, he'll forget about Sunnington and get back on a ship.'

'He'll never do that. He has to find

his father. He thinks he is locked up in the Gorebeck asylum.' Annie wondered if she should confide in her father that she now suspected Colonel Sanderson was behind the scheme, too.

'He is quite right. But he doesn't know that his own Uncle Hughe was the man who put him there with the help of Vickers.'

Annie was appalled.

'Then he could be in great danger, because Benedict Stockyard could be involved also. He knows where Robert's father is and that he will try to find out. How can I warn him, Father?'

'Annie, lass, I think he already will have figured it out, don't you? But what choice does he have?'

'Father, you are safe here. I need to . . . ' Annie stood up and kissed her father's cheek.

He grabbed her arm firmly.

'Listen and listen good. That lamp oil was spilled on the step in the lighthouse for a reason. It was a warning to me. It could have cost either of us our lives. I refused to put out the light in a storm and although I turned many a blind eye to goods being landed, lass, I'd never cause a ship to hit the rocks for the likes of Vickers. I'm not sayin' smuggling's right, but by the heck, I'd never be a party to wreckin'. Now, we were lucky last time. Don't you cross these people or you'll end up in their trade.'

'I'd never join them, you know me better that that,' Annie answered indignantly.

'Annie, the London lot, they deal in anything — opium, liquor, arms and women. You wouldn't join them tradin' like, you'd be part of the goods they'd sell. They wouldn't waste a bullet on a pretty young lass, they'd use and sell you in the dens of London, or worse, abroad.'

Annie's mouth dropped open. She had never heard of such evil and to think it had spread as far as Ebton frightened and sickened her in equal measures.

She was lost for words, when Betty

knocked on the door to tell her that her bath was ready.

Annie bade a polite goodbye to her father.

'Think carefully on what I have told you, Annie.' He forced a smile.

'Yes, Father.' Annie made herself smile brightly back at him and left.

As she sank into the warm tub, which Betty had prepared for her, and closed her eyes she decided Nellie would know how to warn Zachariah, but could even Nellie be trusted?

As the water eased her body, despite her thoughts, she started to feel relaxed and clean. She had even decided to heed her father's words. It was only when she stood up and wrapped a towel around her refreshed body that she saw the adjoining bedroom door close. Her clean body immediately felt dirty once more.

Someone had been watching her. She ran over to the door and opened it slightly but the room was empty. She closed it and turned the key.

9

Zachariah rode like the devil himself was on his tail. He took a cross-country route that dissected the Sunnington estate. His memory of it was as clear as if he had ridden the land only yesterday. It was exhilarating to gallop freely across the place he should and would rightfully consider his own.

Benedict had recognised him, but if he would not willingly relinquish what he had been unduly given, then Zachariah realised he and his father were in grave danger. Yet something was missing from this scenario. Benedict had always cheated at cards and been a liar, but he was basically incapable of thinking for himself, which is why he had had to cheat. So who was behind this madness? It could not have been Uncle Hughe, unless his untimely death was an accident. The matter troubled him as he rode into the cover of a croft. From here he could see clear to Gorebeck and back to the coast road as it skirted Stangcliffe.

Far in the distance he saw a coach and some soldiers. Zachariah estimated that, if he rode straight to Gorebeck, the riders would be an hour behind if, in fact, they were going to the same destination. He wasted no time. He entered the town through its main square. The small market town had a few fine buildings, a prominent Norman church, a smattering of shops and some higgledy-piggledy houses that ran down to a river. Beyond this and over a bridge was built the ominous asylum. He made for it quickly.

Once at its gates he entered the cobbled, grimy yard. This, as he suspected, was a sombre, dour place. His stomach knotted in a fit of anger and disgust at the thought that his strong, proud and gentlemanly father could be held here.

'Good day, sir. Now what can we be

doin' for you, do you think?'

The voice came from the shadows of an out building. It was a man's voice, deep and rough, and something sounded almost familiar about it.

'I am here to visit Lord Thomas Algernon Stockyard Esquire. I believe he is a patient of the establishment.'

Zachariah dismounted and stood next to the horse holding the reins firmly. He dropped his hand to his side near his loaded pistol.

'Who are you, sir?' the voice asked from the shadows.

'Show yourself, man, and I shall answer your questions,' Zachariah said and watched as, slowly out of every corner of the yard, men came forward until five of them surrounded him, all carrying loaded pistols. Then the voice spoke once more as a large figure of a man came forward, wearing the high boots and a great oilskin cape coat that accentuated his build.

'Selwyn Fletcher! What on earth are you doing here? I thought you fished the coast south of Hull?' Zachariah asked as he looked at the scarred face of his once fellow seaman. Once, because, if it had not been for Zachariah, the man would have been hanged from the yardarm three years since. Zachariah had given the man a fighting chance if he could swim ashore. Selwyn was as strong as an ox and the sea had been kind to him that day.

'We have a problem, Mr Zachariah Rudd, sir, and you're it.'

Selwyn walked over to Zachariah and spoke quietly.

'I've orders to kill you and your father. Eradicate the problem like.'

Selwyn scratched the stubble on his chin as if deep in thought.

'Whose orders? Benedict's?' Zachariah said not believing it were possible.

'No, the man's a sop. No. Jebidiah Vickers, a hard man, Zach. Not a gent like you and meself.' Selwyn chuckled and walked Zach and the horse over to the shadows; his men faded into the darkness also.

'Ignore them. I can help you more than this man Vickers. Help me sort out this mess and then I'll be in a position to help you.' Selwyn looked at him thoughtfully. 'I saved your life, man. Does that stand for nothing?' Zachariah asked.

'Aye, it does. But you're asking me to save yours, yer father's and risk me own into the bargain.'

'You know I'm Robert Stockyard,' Zachariah said and the man shifted uneasily.

'Aye, I do, God help me. It was my father who was paid by yer uncle to organise the press-gang. Times were hard, lad. And it weren't as if he wanted yer murdered. You've had a good life.'

'Not the one I was born to have, though!' Zachariah snapped.

'Well, maybe not, but you've still done better than most.'

'Then you owe me twice over. Help me free my father and I'll help you rid yourself of this Vickers man.' Zachariah knew it made sense. Selwyn was bent but not evil.

'We have orders to take you and your father away to the moors. This we'll do. Then we'll talk again.' Selwyn ordered his men to mount up ready and then he walked Zachariah up to the front door. He hammered hard on it and when it opened a matron wrapped in a soiled apron and carrying a large ring of keys stood gaping at the barrel of Selwyn's raised pistol.

'Take us to Stockyard!' Selwyn ordered, and the woman nearly dropped her keys, her hands were shaking so much with fear. She ran off down a long corridor of bare brick walls. They passed many locked and bolted doors as they went. The pitiful moans and raucous laughter were soul-destroying to Zachariah's ears.

'We should make her open the doors to all of them,' he said angrily.

'No, man. Some of them are as mad as hatters. They'd murder normal God-fearin' folk.' Selwyn looked nervous also.

'You believe demons have possessed them? Ask yourself how your mind would be if you were kept in such stark conditions, your very liberty withdrawn from you, for years on end.'

The woman stopped at a door at the end of the corridor. She turned the key and stepped back.

Zachariah peered in. A small oil lamp glowed on a sparse table. Next to it a fragile-looking figure, dressed in clothes that had been made for man of a more substantial figure, sat reading a book — the Bible.

The man, unshaven, looked up at his visitors. It took a moment for his eyes to focus on the three figures. Then his stare returned to Zachariah. Slowly the Bible that he had held slipped from the man's hands landing on the stone slabbed floor.

'Father, it is I, Robert.' Zachariah crouched in front of him.

'Robert? It can't be . . . can it?' the man's voice was little more than a whisper.

'Yes, well, this is all very heart-warmin'' but could yer pick him up and let's get out of here, afore the yeomanry join us?' Selwyn waited for Zachariah to pick up his father and carry him out before he locked the old woman in. She screamed but like all the other screaming people, she was ignored, her voice lost in the melee, her pleas unheeded.

There was no time to speak. Zachariah nestled his father to him and they rode, surrounded by Selwyn's men, up on to the moor road.

They took cover in the copse and saw the carriage turn off the coast road heading for Gorebeck.

'We had best stick to the old pony tracks and head into the cover of Pelham Woods. The old hermit's cave will hide us from the likes of them, but not for long from Vickers' men. We might try the old inn. You best have a good plan, Zach, if you want to save both your necks.'

'I thought you were Robert.'

His father spoke, but the man's eyes

were looking up at the sky as if he had already been released into the glory of heaven.

'I am, Father. I'll explain when we're safe again.' Zachariah looked at Selwyn. 'And we will all be safe again.'

Selwyn laughed and they rode off at a gallop towards the shelter of the woods.

★ ★ ★

Annie slipped back along the dark, wood-panelled landing to her father's bedroom. She wanted to make sure that the draught the doctor had given him had worked. Annie could only face what she was about to do if she knew her father wasn't lying in bed fretting and making himself ill. Her father's words of warning had scared her.

Annie knew nothing of the world of which he spoke, but she also knew it was against the will of God and wrong. It had to be stopped. Zachariah or Robert, whoever he really was, was their only hope of bringing these men of evil to book.

The doctor had told her that her father's heart was feeling tired and he needed good rest in order to recover its strength. That was something he would not do voluntarily so he was being made to rest by the use of laudanum. Annie saw that he was sleeping soundly and then made her way to the main staircase.

'Well, my dear child, wherever do you think you are going, Annie?'

The portly figure of Aunt Amelia appeared from her room, almost as if she had been watching Annie.

'I was going for a walk, Aunt Amelia. I feel I need some fresh air. It has been a very tiresome morning.' She smiled at the dour figure in front of her.

'If, Annie, it has been a tiresome time, then you must go to your room and rest.' The acidic tone in her aunt's voice hurt Annie but she did not show it. This humourless woman was all the family she had, except for her loving father. 'Then I would advise you to make yourself ready for the colonel's return. He has indeed been most generous and charitable to you. It is time you showed him some gratitude.' Her aunt raised her head and eyebrow and stared pointedly at Annie.

'Aunt Amelia, I have always been polite to the colonel,' Annie said innocently.

'I have no idea what a man in his position should see in a girl more acquainted with fisherwomen, but he has some sort of affection for you. I strongly suggest you nurture it. Your father would be better served at Colonel Sanderson's manor house. He deserves to be in Saint Bart's Hospice rather than depending on my husband's, your dear Uncle Ruben's, charity. We are not a hospital!'

'Neither is that sham of a hovel called Saint Bart's. Surely you would not entertain placing your own brother in such a place.'

Annie was both angry and shocked

by her aunt's attitude. The so-called hospital was the fear of all the townsfolk. Hardly anyone who went in there came out again, certainly not in a healthy state. The doctor who ran it spent more time at the inn than in his wards. Amelia was obviously trying to blackmail Annie into accepting the colonel. Annie was having none of it.

'Young lady, this is our home. If my brother is so foolish as to keep falling over his own feet, then perhaps God is telling him to pull himself together or suffer the consequences!' Her aunt had coloured and Annie realised that she had no love or conscience towards the care of her own brother, at all.

'I can assure you, Aunt Amelia, we will not stay here a moment longer than is absolutely necessary,' Annie replied sharply.

'Nonsense child, you must stay with us until Samuel is strong enough to leave on his own two feet. I am sending for a suitable garment for you to wear for dinner with the colonel and your uncle tonight.'

Amelia smiled, and Annie thought for a moment that she was going mad. Her aunt's manner had changed so suddenly.

'I am returning to Ebton, ma'am. Your man has readied the buggy. I shall be glad to give your instructions to the establishment of Messeurs Blenkinsop.'

Dr Bevin's voice surprised Annie. He must have appeared from the servants' stairwell behind her. Both the colonel and the doctor appeared to be very familiar with her aunt's house.

'You're so kind, sir. I shall write a note forthwith.' Amelia started to descend the main staircase.

Annie quickly regained her composure. She needed to act quickly if she were to stand any chance of contacting Nellie in time to help Zachariah.

'Dear Aunt, I am touched by your kindness and shall fetch my cloak forthwith,' Annie said brightly, like a dutiful niece anxious to go out on a shopping spree.

'Why ever would you do that, Annie?' her aunt asked impatiently.

'To choose a suitable garment and have any adjustments made. There is no time to send it back should it not fit, Aunt.' Annie saw a flash of anger cross her Aunt Amelia's face.

'You cannot possibly burden Dr Bevin with your presence, girl, and I cannot leave the house when my dear brother lays ill a-bed. Besides, how would you return? No, it is out of the question. We must think of your good name.'

Annie pouted for the first time in her life and looked with big round appealing eyes at the doctor. She hated herself for doing it but was desperate to get back to Ebton. Nellie knew everyone. She was the only person Annie could think of who would know how to help Zachariah.

'Miss Darton would be no trouble at all. I shall escort her to the milliner, and then she can take tea with my good lady wife whilst I see to my business. I shall have her escorted back safely Mrs Hammond, have no fear. I am a respected doctor and old enough to be her father. I will gladly chaperone her, Mrs Hammond.'

The doctor smiled and her aunt could only give her permission, so reluctantly she wrote a note to ask for the bill for the dress and accessories to be send to Hammond Hall.

The doctor bowed and stepped out to the waiting buggy. Annie intended to follow but her aunt caught her arm and, with her back to the door, snapped her words out quietly and sharply to Annie.

'You may think you are clever, Annie Darton, but you are a little fool! I'm warning you, girl, Ebton is no place for a young woman to be on her own.'

'But I shall be with the doctor, Aunt,' Annie said calmly.

'You are as stubborn as that imbecile who lays in the bed upstairs. Remember, the colonel is your way out of that hovel and into a decent bed, girl!'

'That is hardly how I would describe a bed with the colonel in it!' Annie whispered, then fastened her cloak around her and placed her bonnet on her head. She ignored her aunt's gasp at her words, and took the small reticule from her with the milliner's note in it and some coins.

'Yes, thank you, Aunt. I shall remember your advice and budget. You are so generous.' Annie had raised her voice because the doctor was looking across at them waiting for Annie to join him.

He helped Annie up then seated himself next to her. He did not speak until they left the hall and were on the open road.

'So, Miss Darton, what finery are you to buy?'

'I am to dine with Colonel Sanderson tonight at dinner and have no suitable dress to wear,' Annie explained but thought he must be desperate to make conversation with her, as he already knew this.

146

'It is a shame I could not take you to York. The shops there sell the finest silks and the ladies undergarments are exquisite.' He was watching her shocked expression that he should comment on such things.

'I'm sure they are, but I wouldn't know,' Annie replied then looked out at the passing countryside, only to have her attention jolted abruptly back to the doctor as he placed a firm hand on her thigh. She let out a gasp.

'Remove that at once, sir!' she ordered.

'Don't be so shocked, Annie. I'm a doctor. I see all manner of things, from the tattered rags of the poor and their emaciated forms, to the beauty of a voluptuous maid, pink, clean and untouched.' He gently squeezed her leg.

Annie stared into the pale grey eyes of this respected figure and could not stop the accusation from leaving her lips.

'It was you who watched me bathe!' She looked at his hand, still clasping her leg through the fabric of her dress.

'Of course it was. And may I say, Miss Annie Darton, you are blessed with a fine body. I wish I were a free man, I'd snap you up this very day!'

'No, sir, you may not. Unhand me and kindly stop this conversation, now!' Annie was livid, but could do nothing, trapped as she was within the buggy.

'I apologise. I thought you may be more worldly than you apparently are. Forget the ramblings of a disheartened old dreamer and be proud you are a beautiful specimen of womanhood. The colonel is a very lucky man.'

Annie wanted to rebel but decided that if the doctor thought she was already spoken for by the colonel, then he would leave her alone. He patted her leg then removed his hand and the rest of the journey was passed with sporadic outbursts of polite conversation. It was with great relief that Annie alighted and entered the milliner's shop.

The doctor said he would allow her half-an-hour to make her choice and then send for her. Annie nodded and then looked wide-eyed at the choice of fabric and the few made-up sample dresses that she would have to find a suitable selection from.

'Could you make it an hour, sir?' she asked.

He smiled and said, 'Three quarters, my dear — no more.'

Once he left, Annie found a day dress that fitted her and asked if she could try it on along with her chosen new undergarments, stockings and boots. Then she quickly found a dress that she was told would be suitable for dinner. Ebton could offer her the choice of two made-up ones in her size.

The lady complained bitterly that they were her samples and normally ladies had dresses made weeks in advance. Annie did not care for it as it was not at all practical but accepted the choice and told them to have it wrapped for her, ready to return with her to the hall. Then she excused herself on the basis that she had to see a friend, but assured the lady that she would return shortly, before the doctor did.

'What, Miss Darton, do you wish done with these?' The rather pompous lady was pointing to Annie's old dress and stockings and worn-out boots.

'Why, wrap them up also, of course!' Annie answered in a similar tone, then she quickly left and headed straight for Nellie's cottage.

Wrapping her old cloak around her and fixing her bonnet on firmly against the sea breeze, Annie ran to the two old familiar cottages. Without knocking on Nellie's door she burst in.

'Nellie, I must talk to you. I don't have long to explain.'

'Come and join us, lass. Why don't yer make yersel' at home?' There was something about Nellie's manner that told Annie she had just made a big mistake.

Nellie was sitting smoking her pipe. The door slammed closed behind her.

'You ain't ever met Jebidiah afore,

have yer, lass?' Nellie asked, but knew the answer too well.

Annie turned and saw a huge, scarred man standing in front of the door.

'Sorry, Nellie, I didn't realise you had company. I'll speak to you later, when I'm not intruding.'

'You ain't goin' nowhere, lass. You're staying right here with me,' Jebidiah leered.

10

Robert and his father were taken firstly to the copse then on to the moors. They were led to the back of a derelict coaching inn on the moor road.

Selwyn dismounted and gestured for Robert to carry his father indoors.

'You can put me down, son. I'm not devoid of the stamina to stand on my own two feet.'

His father grinned. He had lost so much weight that, to Robert, he was a shadow of the man he had always been brought up to respect.

Lord Stockyard wrapped his arms around his son and hugged him for the first time in his life. Robert was touched and shaken by the humbleness and emotion displayed by his father.

'So, you are a Stockyard, Zachariah?' Selwyn said, as he held a pistol pointing at the two of them. 'How strange fate is that where my father arranged for the boy to be removed, the man he grew up into should have saved his own son's skin.'

'Yes. Zachariah Rudd was a name forced upon me, Robert Stockyard, when I was unlawfully pressed into HMS Navy.'

Robert was standing slightly in front of his father, facing Selwyn.

'What to do now?' Selwyn scratched his beard. 'Jebidiah gave me strict instructions to rid this world of the pair of you. He's a very angry man, and gets real upset if folk don't do his biddin'.'

'We can rid you of him, and set you on the right path again, Selwyn,' Robert said.

'Now how could you be doin' that when I've never been on the right path in me life afore?' Selwyn laughed at his own wit.

'Firstly, we must find Dr Harpham who signed the original papers to obtain my father's release.'

Lord Stockyard interrupted, 'Then

we must visit my solicitor to establish my affairs again. Next, we must depose Hughe, the blackguard who I am ashamed to call my own blood brother! I shall see him thrown in jail for the murder of my dear wife and kidnapping of my only son. He'll have his just rewards.'

Robert put his hand on his father's arm because he was almost shaking with rage.

'Uncle Hughe was killed in a riding accident, Father,' Robert said calmly, but Selwyn laughed.

'Accident, my foot! Jebidiah had him removed. Your uncle did not want to settle for his share of the trade. He wanted control of it. Jebidiah never negotiates control. Hughe Stockyard thought he was a hard man, but he wasn't. If he'd been of Vickers' calibre he'd have had you murdered and fed to the gulls. Now the whelp, Benedict, he was too scared to say owt. So old Jeb took out the uncle, so the son was no problem. That's how he solves his problems, like. And that is how he'll solve me if I don't stick a bullet through yer brains here and now.' Selwyn raised the pistol.

'Damn you, man!' Robert snapped. 'I saved your life and I can save your skin now, too! Don't you realise the power a man in my father's position has?'

Selwyn lowered the pistol slightly.

'If you help us now to obtain my father's release papers, we can rid the coast of Jebidiah and his gang of thugs, but we need your help now in order to do it. Or do you want to live in his shadow for ever?'

'How do you know he isn't possessed or insane? After all this time he might be?' Selwyn peered at Lord Thomas.

Lord Stockyard stepped forward and Selwyn raised the pistol again keeping him firmly in his sights.

'I'll have you know that the good Lord has been my strength — that and the knowledge that this day would come when those guilty of the destruction of my family shall be brought to justice!'

Selwyn grinned. 'Well, m'lord, you sound sane to me. Now let's go get a piece of paper signed to say it and you can take the hall back. How d'you suppose we sort out Jebidiah?' Selwyn was asking Robert.

'We need the yeomanry,' Lord Stockyard replied.

'Your Lordship has been away too long. Yer need the Dragoons and the Preventative Officer, William Rusk,' Selwyn answered.

'The yeomanry are fine men. I picked them myself with the guidance of Colonel Sanderson.'

Selwyn laughed.

'Times and folk change; they adapt to survive. Just like you did in that hell hole.' He turned and shouted for one of his men. 'Send your message with Fisher, he'll ride to the barracks.'

Robert spoke to the man who promptly left. Two other men were sent to fetch the doctor and a solicitor from Gorebeck.

In the hour it took for the men to return, Robert told his father roughly where he had been over the long missing years of his father's incarceration. He was not a violent man by nature but Robert wanted nothing less than to see the man, Jebidiah, swing at the end of a rope. How many lives had the wretch destroyed?

When Dr Harpham arrived at gunpoint and was brought into the dilapidated inn, before anybody else could prevent him, Lord Stockyard swung a punch and knocked him down flat.

Robert stepped between the two whilst his father regained his composure and Selwyn helped the stunned medic to his feet, obviously delighted by his lordship's reaction.

★ ★ ★

'Is this the lass who was in the lighthouse with her father?' Jebidiah asked Nellie.

'Yep, she could solve yer problem tonight. She knows all about how it works, don't yer, girl?' Nellie pointed her pipe at Annie.

'But it's working fine. Colonel Sanderson has two men in there now,' Annie answered, staring at Nellie, wondering if the old woman was in league with the dreaded man, Vickers, or if she could still trust her. If she couldn't, it would appear all would be lost.

'Aye, that's right. But I don't want it worked proper.' Vickers moved towards her and bent down to face her. His breath stank, his skin was oily and his eyes showed only evil. Annie wanted to run. Her father's words came flooding back to her. What had she done?

'I want it to go out, just when I needs it to. There's a ship coming this way tonight. One that I'd like to stop here for a visit — a permanent one!'

He and Nellie laughed and Annie felt sick to her stomach. Like her father she would never be a party to a wreck.

'I'm sorry to disappoint you but I have an engagement in twenty minutes with the good doctor and then with Colonel Sanderson at the hall tonight. My absence would raise the alarm and your plan would be sadly foiled.' Annie forced herself to stay calm and stare this man straight in the eye.

'Is that so, miss?' Vickers exclaimed then laughed.

'Let me go about my business and I'll say no more about it,' Annie said as confidently as she could.

'No, somehow I don't think so.' A knock on the door made Annie jump. It was a pattern of three gentle knocks followed by two loud ones. Vickers opened it and Dr Bevin came in.

'Oh, I see you've met, Miss Darton.' Dr Bevin doffed his hat to her.

'You know this man, doctor?' Annie asked; her stomach had an awful sinking feeling.

'Oh, yes. This is Mr Vickers. He is quite a man of business in these parts, aren't you, Jebidiah?' Dr Bevin stood in front of Nellie and she quickly evacuated her favourite chair. The doctor sat down by the fire.

'Colonel Sanderson isn't involved in any of this at all, is he?' Annie asked in disbelief, and caught a sharp warning glance from Nellie.

'Sweet child,' the doctor started to reply then grinned and pulled on Annie's skirt so she stumbled a step towards him. 'But you're not a child, are you? We've established that already, haven't we?'

Annie stepped back but rebounded off Vickers who was now standing behind her. The doctor pulled her on to his lap and placed his arms tightly around her. She started to kick out but Vickers pinned her legs firmly.

Annie hadn't noticed until that point that Maude was crouched in the corner. She saw her edge around to the door. Annie knew she had to cause a distraction if Maude was to get out of there and help her. Surely Maude would, even if Nellie was as hard as nails.

'Let me go,' Annie shouted. 'The colonel will look for me!'

She was almost screaming as they tightened their grip on her as she struggled. The doctor planted his mouth over hers but she bit his lip. He threw her to the floor, raised his hand to strike her, but Vickers grabbed it.

'Think, man, don't damage the goods.'

Vickers looked at the door as it shut behind Maude.

He looked at Nellie.

'Fetch the old fool back here this minute! D'ye hear!'

''Tis all right. Maude is frightened of her own shadow. She'll go find a safe hole to hide in till yer finished, like.' Nellie was squatting, calmly sucking her pipe.

'Aye, perhaps so. But you'll answer if yer wrong,' Vickers replied, before grabbing hold of Annie and standing her in front of the doctor again.

He was wiping away a trickle of blood from his lip.

'Sanderson couldn't even run a yeomanry guard. He's an old fool who has a yearning for a young woman, who he loves. Sad really, because she couldn't give a care for him. But it is very convenient for us, because now we have you, dear Annie. He will at last turn a blind eye to things that he has interfered with in the past. You are goin' to help us this night in more ways than one.' The doctor turned as if he were going to walk away, then struck her across her face. Annie's face stung but Vickers had a firm hold on her.

'Now, we will make our way to the lighthouse. You will tell the men there how to lure the ship on to the rocks and then, my girl, you will be reunited with the colonel.'

'Never!' she screamed. 'I would rather die!'

The doctor laughed and said calmly, 'Your wish might be granted; however, that will come in our time, not yours, but, yes, by the time we have finished with you I can assure you, you might prefer it.'

Vickers' hands held her body firmly and Annie wriggled and struggled but to no avail. He threw her over his shoulder as if she were no more than a child and then headed out of the door and through the dunes towards the light.

11

'There, our business is complete, sir.' Lord Stockyard held the papers that he had dreamed of in his hand — or had nightmares about over the last few years.

'I prayed this day would come.'

'Sir, I'm heartily sorry. They threatened my family,' Dr Harpham snivelled and tried to explain. It was not the first time that Lord Stockyard had had him before him begging his forgiveness for his part in the fall of the Stockyard family. Each time Thomas had wanted to punch the man but, because he was trapped, he could not. Now, having vented his initial anger on him, he could not find it in his heart to hate him anymore. Forgive him? No, he couldn't do that either but, feel pity for the guilt-ridden wretch? Yes.

'Go back to your family, man, and be

grateful you still have one.' The doctor almost ran to the door. 'But think on this. When I am restored to my home and position, I shall be writing to the inspectors about the state of your asylum and I shall have it closed, and you condemned for abuse, unless you change radically the way you treat those luckless souls.'

The doctor nodded frantically and ran to his horse, galloping away without looking back.

Mr Giles, the Gorebeck solicitor, saw that the papers were in order.

'This is by far the oddest business I have ever seen conducted, your lord-ship.'

'Have no worries, your time will be well rewarded. You shall receive my monetary gratitude very shortly and I am sure it shall not be found wanting,' Lord Stockyard said to the man as he left. Robert admired the decorum of his father. After all these years being locked away like an animal he was still every inch a gentleman.

'Where to now, gents?' Selwyn asked.

'To my rightful home, to see the wretch that is my only nephew.' Robert helped his father on to his horse then jumped up behind him. Together they rode straight for Sunnington Hall. There was no sign of the colonel's coach.

'He must have returned when he found you were not there,' Selwyn said.

'I cannot believe that Sanderson would be in on such foul play as this,' Lord Stockyard commented.

'He wasn't. He's been led a wild dance by his men and Dr Bevin, not to mention Vickers. It's only because young Robert here returned that gossip started up and he finally started piecing together what has been happenin' around here for years.'

Robert looked across at Selwyn.

'Then if he's not a part of this why is he pestering Annie?'

'Who is Annie?' Lord Stockyard asked.

'Because he wants her, and he has

thoughts her father was summit to do with Vickers. Someone was whisperin' untruths in his ear to keep him guessing.'

Robert broke into a gallop. He wanted to get his father established at Sunnington, sort out Benedict and had a burning desire to rescue Annie from Sanderson's clutches.

Robert steadied his father as he put his feet down on the ground outside his own home.

'Sunnington Hall,' his father spoke the words softly. He looked as though he was so moved by returning that he may fold in a fit of emotion, but Robert soon realised it was a barely controlled rage.

Robert burst through the hall doors as soon as the servant answered the bell. He ran up the stairs and headed straight for the room that had once been his father's. He smelled the smoke before he entered. He knew it instantly. It sickened him.

He dragged Benedict out of the room

in his shirt and trousers. He protested but so far was he in the opium-induced world of hallucination, he hardly knew what was occurring.

Selwyn had arrived with his men. Robert summoned the staff into the hall and Selwyn had Benedict carried into the lounge.

'Cook, I need good food for my father and a hot drink.'

She nodded and ran to the kitchens. Robert turned to the rest of the staff.

'I want his bedroom stripped and that substance destroyed. This is Lord Stockyard. He is master of Sunnington Hall and you will obey his orders. I am Robert Stockyard, his son and heir. When I return I shall want to know the condition of every aspect of this estate.'

'Selwyn, I need your help. The Dragoons should be on their way to the coast. However, if Vickers has the chance to slip through the net, he will be the bane of our lives. Show me where I can find him.'

Selwyn nodded.

'What about him?' He pointed towards Benedict.

'I'll see to him, just leave me two trustworthy men,' Lord Stockyard said.

Robert nodded. 'He's already in his own living hell anyway, Father. He's an opium addict.'

'Then he will literally rot in it.' Father and son hugged briefly. 'Robert, I have just found you are alive, don't make me face your death again.'

Robert looked at his father with a longing and pride.

'No, Father, I shall be back shortly — with Annie.'

★   ★   ★

Maude ran through the ravine to the coast road. She was frightened. Questions ran through her mind — over and over. What if she told on Jebidiah Vickers? What would he do? Sell her? No, no that was out of the question, she was too old. He might have her locked away as a demon possessed witch!

She finally made it to the open road. If she ran to the south to Hammond Hall she could tell Samuel. Poor, sick Samuel. He couldn't help her. Would his sister? Maude sighed. No, she would be glad to be shot of her.

'Oh, dear!' Maude said out loud. If she ran to the north she would reach Sunnington Hall but Mr Benedict wouldn't let her anywhere near him and, besides, he was as bad as any. No, she had to find Zachariah. She sighed as she thought of the handsome young stranger who was the long lost Robert, son of a lord. It was so romantic and he so handsome. What she would give to be young and pretty like Annie.

'Oh, dear,' she said again as she thought of Annie in the hands of those brutes. She decided to follow the road to Sunnington and then walk on the Gorebeck road. She might bump into him.

Her mind continued on its muddled, depressing tack until she looked up and saw a coach coming towards her from the Gorebeck road. As it neared, she recognised it as the colonel's.

'Praise the Lord!' she sighed in relief. He'd help. The colonel would do anything for Annie.

She waved frantically until the coach slowed down. The lieutenant rode his horse around to her.

'Get out of the way, woman! Stop your begging or I'll run you down.'

Maude looked at him and cursed to herself. He was one of them. She looked down and stepped back.

'What is it woman?' the colonel shouted down.

'A ragamuffin, sir. Nothing to take your attention, sir.'

The lieutenant leered at her and she knew she was in danger. Also, so was Nellie if she did something foolish.

'I'm sorry, sir. Didn't mean no harm. I just felt queasy, like, and panicked that I was havin' a turn. Sorry.'

Maude looked straight up at the colonel and bit her lip nervously.

'Get about your business, wench.'

The lieutenant pushed her with his horse so she had to step back away from the coach.

'Oh, let her up, Carter. We'll drop her off by the Ebton road.'

The colonel released the catch on the door.

'Sir.' The lieutenant wanted to walk around and warn Maude to keep her mouth firmly shut but he was ordered to lead the way, without further interruption, to Hammond Hill via the Ebton road.

Maude looked nervously at the colonel as she sat in the corner of the carriage. She was aware how clean and pretty it was and how dirty she was. She'd never been in a coach before and she fancied herself as a princess and Zachariah as her prince riding along a sun-soaked road where no-one hurt anyone.

'She's been held at Nellie's. She needs your help. The doctor and Vickers are goin' to use her to get at you.' Maude said the words in a barely audible tone.

The colonel stared straight at her and she started quivering. Perhaps he was in on it and she hadn't known. She'd be dead, and never see Nellie again! What had she done?

'You mean Annie, don't you?' the colonel asked.

'Yes, poor Annie.' Maude looked down at her hands in her lap.

'Lieutenant, send word to the barracks to give us back-up. We're going to Ebton!'

Maude panicked and started slapping the colonel's back.

'Not him! Not him! He works with them.'

No sooner were the words out of his mouth than the coach was taken at a gallop along the coast road, without stopping at the Ebton junction. The colonel and Maude were flung together on the back seat as it thundered onwards.

* * *

Annie screamed and wriggled and kicked, without breaking free. Jebidiah carried her onwards to the lighthouse. They passed one of the local men but they just nodded to him and ignored her pleas. Whatever Jebidiah did, no-one challenged or saw. By the time they reached the lighthouse she was nearly exhausted.

He dropped her on the earth at the familiar door.

'Now, lass, get yersel' in there and yer better start deciding to be nice to Jeb or he's goin' to enjoy makin' it not so nice for Miss Annie.' Jebidiah was waving a warning finger at her.

She stopped and caught her breath. She had to keep her head. Once inside the lighthouse she would be trapped. Her only hope was to use her knowledge of the light and the ground around her, to escape.

She stood up slowly and hung her shoulders as if she were submitting to the inevitable.

'That's me girl. Now if yer see sense,

who knows, I might just keep yer for mesel' or share yer with the old colonel. It would be our secret.' He lifted her chin as if admiring her face and she fought with all her might not to bite his hand as his finger followed the contour of her cheeks.

She waited for the right moment. It would come soon; his guard was lowering. She had to make him feel she had seen the wisdom of his words. He was used to controlling people — having them do his bidding for fear of reprisals. That was the way he got what he wanted, but he would not get her.

Now, she thought. With one quick movement, she was over the wall and running through the gorse and out on to the rocks.

She heard a string of expletives from Vickers' mouth. He had attempted to follow her over the wall, but where she had played around this headland all her life, he only knew the coast from the sea. He nearly slipped and called out for his men to come out of the lighthouse and follow her.

She did not look back but was concentrating on working her way down to the cave beneath. If the tide was far enough out, she would be able to get back to the bay. If his men were there, then she would have to take her chance on the rocks. He would never have her — never!

She heard a deathly scream as one of her pursuers fell to his death. In the moment she had paused to see what had happened, the second man caught her up.

'Amos!' she was shocked that Seth's son would go with Jebidiah. 'Not you, too!'

'No, you damn stupid wench. What the hell do yer think yer was doin'? Didn't yer aunt tell yer to stay home. The colonel told her to.' Amos grabbed her and pulled her behind a boulder, out of sight.

'Yes, but she didn't say the colonel had said so. Anyway, I thought he was up to something with Vickers. I heard him talking to the butler in the hall,' Annie explained but was surprised when he grinned at her.

'That's William Rusk the Preventative Officer. He's been placed there in disguise to try to find out once and for all who at the hall has been connected with Jebidiah. It turned out it wasn't yer uncle but the good doctor.' He spat his disgust over the rock face.

'They thought I hanged King. I agreed to help them wind Vickers' group up, as they was prepared to let me swing for killing the swine. Then your friend, Zachariah, turned up and blew the whole thing wide open. Nobody expected Robert to return from the dead. But it provided the missing link. But yer couldn't stay put, could yer?'

He started pushing at a large rock in front of them.

'What are you doin'?' Annie asked.

'Savin' yer life. Now scream.' Amos gave it a hard push.

'Aghh . . . ' Annie screamed and

released all her fear and indignation that was trapped within her.

The rock broke free. 'Stop.'

There was a loud splash. 'Then he said, ''Scuse me, miss,' and ripped a part of the sleeve off her dress.

'Now stay here as long as yer can. I'll tell him yer slipped and hope he don't blow out me brains.'

He started to climb back up to the lighthouse and Annie hugged her legs to her. She was cold, frightened and worried. What had happened to Zachariah?

'You fool, I should skin yer!' Vickers' yell rang out over the seagulls' call. 'Yer let her drop, didn't yer?'

'I couldn't help it. She struggled like crazy.' Amos didn't have time to hear Jebidiah's response as Zachariah galloped up to the light and dismounted. Vickers went for his pistol but, in his distraction with Amos, was too slow. Zachariah threw himself from this horse on to Vickers, knocking him to the ground. The huge man punched Zach in the stomach, but he had fought many times and could take a beating.

They rolled over the rough ground and, as the gradient increased, they were thrown apart. Both stood up.

'Where is she?' Zachariah asked. Behind him he heard the colonel's coach pull up.

The lieutenant was going to come to Vickers' aid but the colonel pulled a gun on him and told him he'd shoot him dead if he took one more step. They had already seen the Dragoons in the distance.

'Where is she?' Zachariah repeated.

Jebidiah laughed at him.

'Why, you must be Robert Stockyard Esquire. Well, well. Didn't Miss Annie make a killin' in her short life.' He looked from one to the other as he propped himself on the wall. 'Broke the heart of a young gent, an old fool and meself into the bargain.'

'What do you mean?' the colonel asked Vickers.

Maude sneaked out of the carriage,

her hand to her mouth.

'Why, nothing unfortunately,' Vickers sighed. 'Come, I'll take yer to her.' He put his leg over the wall. 'She's waitin' fer yer down here.' He beckoned Zachariah to come to him.

'I'm here.'

When Annie's voice answered him, Vickers stood up, but one single shot from the colonel's pistol caused him to fall over into the gorse. Zachariah pulled Annie to safety. She held him tightly.

'Oh, Zach. I wanted to help you,' Annie explained.

'You did, Annie,' the colonel's voice answered her. 'Look in Vicker's left hand. The blackguard was about to put a small pistol bullet through your friend's heart.'

'Colonel, I am Robert Stockyard. I thank you for saving my life. You shot him but your wayward lieutenant has escaped,' Robert answered and pointed to the figure making off on his borrowed horse.

'He won't get far. The Dragoons will soon have him. But what do we do now, Annie?' the colonel asked.

'Dr Bevin is the real brains behind this operation. He has been all along,' Annie explained but need not have.

'He has been arrested and is already on his way to York. It looks as though you will be needing yet another new dress, Miss Darton,' the colonel said.

'There is no need of further charity. I shall take care of Miss Darton from this day forth,' Robert answered the older man.

'No need for either of your charity,' Maude said as she appeared from the lighthouse carrying a small box.

'Samuel Darton left his safe box in the lighthouse when he left so sudden like, and he hadn't been able to get back in since then.' She gave the box to Annie who nestled it to her. She had no bonnet. That had flown to the winds, her dress was torn and her skirts ripped and stained. Yet, she smiled because now she understood why her father had

had a fixation on the lighthouse. He wasn't pining for it, but trying to figure out how to get back inside.

'Allow me to escort you back to Hammond Hall, Miss Darton.'

'Thank you, colonel.'

'Maude, how did you know where it was?' Annie asked.

Maude just winked.

'Miss Maude, would you care for a ride back, too?' the colonel asked and she nodded excitedly.

'Well, Miss Darton, I must return to Sunnington and attend my father. He needs me.'

Annie nodded and, as the colonel helped Maude into the carriage, she turned to him. 'Zachariah . . . '

'Miss Darton, Annie. May Robert call on you tomorrow and give his thanks to your father?' he smiled broadly at her.

'Yes, he may.'

'May Robert Stockyard call on you . . . often?' He looked into her eyes and she wanted nothing more than him to call on her all the time.

'Yes, he may.'

'Then he will look forward to his visits eagerly, with anticipation.' He bent over and kissed her hand. 'Your carriage awaits you, Annie.'

Annie stepped inside then spoke to the colonel.

'Thank you for saving him for me.'

He looked charmingly at her and simply replied, 'What are friends for, Miss Darton, and I hope always to be your friend.'

'I'm sure you always will be.'

The coach rolled on and Maude chuckled quietly to herself.

THE END

We do hope that you have enjoyed reading this large print book.

Did you know that all of our titles are available for purchase?

We publish a wide range of high quality large print books including:
Romances, Mysteries, Classics
General Fiction
Non Fiction and Westerns

Special interest titles available in large print are:
The Little Oxford Dictionary
Music Book, Song Book
Hymn Book, Service Book

Also available from us courtesy of Oxford University Press:
Young Readers' Dictionary
(large print edition)
Young Readers' Thesaurus
(large print edition)

For further information or a free brochure, please contact us at:
Ulverscroft Large Print Books Ltd.,
The Green, Bradgate Road, Anstey,
Leicester, LE7 7FU, England.
Tel: (00 44) **0116 236 4325**
Fax: (00 44) **0116 234 0205**

SO GOLDEN THEIR HARVEST

Jane Carrick

Susan and Hazel had looked after their father since their mother's death, but now Susan is to marry Colin, a farmer, and move to Australia. However, after Colin's Gran has a fall, the old lady begs him to take over her run-down farm in Scotland instead. Susan doesn't mind and works hard with Colin to build up the farm. Peter, one of the farm hands, falls in love with Susan, but she has eyes only for Colin. When Hazel visits Susan, she finds herself attracted to the handsome Peter, but he tells her of his love for her sister.